LOTTERY OF LIES

A PSYCHOLOGICAL THRILLER

NADIJA MUJAGIC

CHAPTER 1

LYNN

IF THE OCEAN COULD TALK, it would reveal that my husband, Jimmy, lies at its depths, being consumed by sharks and fish. Thankfully, my secret lies safely at the bottom of it.

The only other person who knows I've murdered Jimmy is Skull, my former drug dealer and longstanding friend. But Skull won't tell anyone, as I hired and paid him a lot of money to keep his mouth shut. I've entrusted him with my life. He's reliable and professional, and he's never given me any problems.

Have I thought of coming forward and confessing to the police? Sure. The idea has crossed my mind many times, but every time I've come to the same conclusion: the secret must stay. This year has been a whirlwind of turning events and emotions, and I've won the jackpot, literally and figuratively, so I don't want my luck to go to waste.

Now, my life is a dream. As of today, I live in a

spacious house along the ocean with my long-lost daughter, Lucy. Can it get any better? I somehow doubt it.

Living in this expansive house has come with a few considerations. We'll need to hire house cleaners, gardeners, a repairman, and anyone else necessary to maintain this intricate and large place. Lucy and I simply don't have the skills required to upkeep our new little mansion. My daughter claims she can cook like no one's business, so there's one thing less to worry about.

We'd needed to iron out a few details with my real estate agent, Cecilia, before we moved in. I'm grateful she didn't return my call to cancel the offer on the house. She told me she hadn't received my voicemail, which, I suppose, is a convenient way to ignore me.

But everything has worked out for the best. We just had to amend the offer to remove Jimmy's name because, as I explained to Cecilia, he and I were on the cusp of a nasty divorce.

"Oh, I'm sorry. And I completely understand. Sometimes, a sudden turn of fortune puts a lot of pressure on couples," Cecilia offered. She didn't probe further, so we left it at that.

We've added Lucy's name to the deed. She will co-own the house, so, if something happens to me, she can be in charge. I promised Lucy she'd be in my will, and the house would be hers too. I wanted to make sure she felt secure and part of the family. Adding her to these important things meant she would always have a place in my heart and our home.

The house came fully furnished and looking like something out of a magazine, featuring the best and the latest. The furniture is modern, the chosen colors complement each other, and the décor is out of this world. It's a place you'd want to spend all your time in, while soaking in its beauty. The previous owners called this a *vacation home*, and maybe it was just one of their vacation homes. I heard they'd sold this house to move onto a better and bigger thing.

Well, I suppose I did the same with mine.

God, I won't miss the tiny row house near the beach where I'd spent decades of my life. That house is a shithole and it's attached to so many horrific memories that still bring me nightmares. Junk removers had picked all the furniture from the house the day I moved. The couch I murdered Jimmy on was finally gone from my sight, and I could relax. I'd kept the old blanket over it, to hide the blood, and added another layer of plastic so everything remained intact during the move. The only piece of evidence gone forever. I'd waved it goodbye, relieved that I would never again have to sit on it. Or that smelly recliner Jimmy used to get drunk in. The only thing I might miss from the old home is our next-door neighbor, Rose. Annoying as she sometimes is, I'd like it if she would come visit occasionally. Unlike before, she'll have to call me to see if I'm home instead of just stumbling in and knocking on my door, unannounced.

We haven't met our new neighbors yet. Will we ever? Our houses are so far apart, separated by lots of land, hedges, and trees. It will be nice to meet them at some point, but it won't be a big deal if I never do. Maybe I'll invite them to our housewarming party that Lucy and I are planning.

But it won't be just a housewarming party. It will be a chance for mine and Lucy's worlds to collide. An opportunity to meet new people.

Excitement pulses through me whenever I think about my daughter and how I now have her by my side. What a great way to start my life anew.

CHAPTER 2

LUCY

OUR TRANSITION to the new house has been smooth. I pinch myself to ensure all of this is real.

All my life I've lived in New Hampshire, but closer to the mountains. My family and I lived in a small colonial built in the 1920s, surrounded by the White Mountains. My adopted dad, Fred, is an insurance agent, and my adopted mom, Mary, worked as a high school teacher until she died. They could afford a colonial house, but not a mansion like this one. Despite our modesty, our house was filled with unparalleled warmth and love.

In the summers, we partook in hiking adventures, and in the winters, we went downhill skiing, only steps away from our house. The ocean wasn't particularly appealing, so we rarely ventured to the east side of the state. Now that I've seen most of it, Hampton is a pleasant town, hopping with tourists in the summer, offering a reprieve from life's humdrum. There are beaches to enjoy, paths to walk, and restaurants to visit. Activities in the small town are abounding, and it's no surprise the town is busy in the summer. Lynn has told me that once the weather cools down around here, the town becomes desolate.

Desolate. I'm okay with that.

Moving into this extravagant mansion has been like stepping into a dream. The walls whisper tales of luxury, and the rooms echo with the promise of a fresh start. It's as if the universe has conspired to bring my mother and me to this place of grandeur. The house smells of freshly painted walls mingled with the lingering fragrance of the previous owners' wealth.

This house energizes me and gives me the proclivity to be the best daughter I can be to Lynn. I want to show how much I appreciate finding her and being by her side. We have a life ahead of us to bond and make up for the days we've lost. She didn't make the best choices in life, I get it, but forgiveness is half the battle. The guilt she has carried for years pushes us to continue building our relationship.

There's no reason to go back.

We walk around the house, delirious, checking every nook and cranny that's now ours. Every now and again we grab each other's arms and shake them in excitement.

"Lucy, darling, can you believe this is ours?" Lynn's eyes sparkle with a mix of disbelief and joy as she surveys the foyer, then walks into the kitchen and spins around like on a Ferris wheel.

I grin, soaking in the moment. "Feels like we've stumbled into a movie set or something."

Lynn laughs. It's the first time I've heard her voice

filled with genuine joy and happiness. The rooms unfold before us like chapters in a fairy tale. The living room is a spectacle of modern elegance, with sleek furniture that practically begs to be lounged on. Lynn's eyes linger on the expansive windows that frame a view of the ocean, then the intricate architectural details of the crown molding edging the ceilings across the entire house.

"Can you believe we get to wake up to this every day?" she muses.

Our bedrooms are no less enchanting. Mine, adorned with shades of lavender and teal, feel like a haven of tranquility. I feel like a princess living in a magical castle. Lynn's room, across from mine, boasts a breathtaking view of the front yard, and seems to reflect her newfound sense of liberation.

The kitchen, a culinary sanctuary awaiting my exploration, holds the promise of countless meals and shared laughter. Lynn, with a glint of undefined mischief in her eyes, comments, "Time to put your claim to fame as a top-notch chef to the test, Lucy."

"Challenge accepted," I respond, touching the state-of-the-art appliances as if made of gold. A new home means new beginnings, and I'm determined to make the most of it.

After suppressing our euphoria, we shift our attention to the logistics of moving into the house. We'd used Lynn's car to haul several boxes to the house. It had been easy because we didn't have a lot of things. As we unpack the boxes, I peek to her side to see what she's taking out.

Mainly clothes, which look old and untasteful. I'll have to go shopping with her. Her attire had left the fashion world a long ago. I crane my neck a little more to discover if she has any valuables to unpack, but there are none.

She turns to me and gives me a frightening stare. "Yes?"

I stop what I'm doing for a second "Hey, I was just wondering if you might have a photo album you can show me. I'd love to see what you and Jimmy looked like when you were young."

She turns in the opposite direction and runs her hand through her hair as if she's thinking. "Umm, you know. I don't know where I've left it. It's somewhere in these boxes." She shoves her hands in one of them and pulls a bunch of shirts out, her arms flying in the air. Perhaps she's searching for the album, but she doesn't seem to be focusing on the task.

"It's okay. Whenever you find it." I pull out my album and place it against my chest, smiling at Lynn. "Do you want to see my photo album? All the photos of me when I was a baby and a young kid?"

Lynn purses her lips and raises her brows. "Yeah, sure. I'd love to see them."

I hand the album to her, and she takes it in slow motion, looking disinterested. She flips the pages and checks out the photos, but she doesn't ask who the other people in the photos are, or how old I was in each. I can't get a word in because her hand moves too swiftly. In most photos, it's my adopted mom or dad standing next to me, holding me and smiling, or giving me a kiss. The photos portray my carefree and glorious past, the childhood my adopted parents gifted me.

Before you know it, Lynn's already done looking at all the photos. She flips to the last page and closes the album before handing it back to me. A fake smile crosses her face. "This is so lovely. Thanks for showing it to me."

We go back to taking things out of the boxes in silence. Her disinterest in my past bothers me, but I suspect Lynn is stressed because of the move and the tasks involved in settling into the new home. But I'm here to turn her life upside down and inside out as we navigate our life together. I wouldn't be surprised if she felt a pang of jealousy about my past and the fact that I have another set of parents who have given me nothing but love. Maybe I need to be more careful about sharing my other parents. It should be all about us know—me and Lynn, connecting and embracing each other.

Time moves at a rapid pace, and before I know it, the sun dips below the horizon, casting hues of pink and gold across the ocean. Lynn and I walk outside to the back of the house, where we inhale a mixture of salt and an ocean breeze. It serves as a reminder that in this new home, we can redefine ourselves, free from the shadows of the past.

"This is our story now, Lucy," Lynn whispers, her gaze fixed on the horizon.

I nod, feeling the weight of our shared journey and the boundless potential ahead. "And it's just beginning, Mom."

IT'S A SUNNY AUGUST DAY, nearly ninety degrees outside. To beat the heat, Lucy and I are hanging inside our new air conditioned home. The ocean breeze hugging the house isn't enough to cool us off. The weather is perfect for staying inside and making plans.

A few days after we moved in, we make plans for our housewarming party. Lucy is excited about organizing it. Ever since we moved in, that's all she's been talking about. We're sitting at the kitchen table making a list of party attendants and brainstorming about food catering.

"Mom, what do you think about this menu?" Lucy pushes a piece of paper across the table, her face beaming. We've been thinking of all the people we want to invite. She's already told me she'd invite everyone she knows: her friends, acquaintances, former co-workers, her adopted family.

It's in a couple of weeks, and we've been putting off the plans for too long. We must decide soon.

I grab the paper and read from the menu. Lucy has carefully curated the food choices, curtesy of Red Urchin. I know their menu by heart, as I worked there for almost thirty years. The menu has changed little over the years, except for some seasonal additions, such as lobster rolls in the summer, or prime rib in the winter.

When Barbara heard of our party, she offered to cater it. For free. When you're out of a toxic marriage, you suddenly realize who your loyal friends are, or that you have them. Barbara has emerged as a good friend, and I've accepted her generous offer and invited all the staff from Red Urchin to our party.

As I look over the menu, I'm impressed with Lucy's choices. In fact, everything she does is impressive. It's incredible to realize she's my own creation, and I'm in awe of the fact that she's turned out decent.

"Nice, Lucy. I really like the choices." I push the menu back in her direction. "I can call Barbara today and let her know what we want."

"Oh, that won't be necessary," Lucy adds, "I've already spoken with Barbara. She agreed to this." She smiles.

My eyes widen and I cock my head to the side. "You did?"

If she did, why is she asking for my opinion now? Why didn't she check in before she called? Does she not need me? I was under the impression we'd be making decisions together.

"I didn't want to bother you. I know how busy you're with everything else." She stands up from the chair and goes to grab a glass of water. "Besides, you really need to learn to rely on me a little more now that I'm here." She drinks her water, making the loud gulping noise while gazing at me over the glass rim. She lets out a long sigh and looks at me, awaiting my response.

My shoulders sag, and I exhale. "I guess. I just need to get used to it. You know, all my life, I've done everything on my own."

She nods. "I know." Lucy approaches me and puts her hand on my shoulder. "Take your time, Mom. Remember, you can count on me."

Music to my ears. I haven't heard someone say anything similar since I was a child. As an only child, my parents used to coddle me and make sure I'm safe and happy, and no one came close after. Jimmy tried, at least in the beginning of our relationship, but once he found comfort in commitment, he couldn't care less.

It will take some getting used to, this new way of living. Lucy is a dream. She's so considerate and kind. Wonderful manners. Would she have been as well put together if Jimmy and I had raised her? If I were to guess, most likely not.

In all honestly, I'm a little nervous about meeting her adopted family and all her friends. She has told me stories about her stepfather, whom she still affectionally calls Daddy, making me cringe. I'm apprehensive about their closeness, as she still seems to cling to him. But that's what exemplary parents do, right? They provide safety for their children in whatever sticky situation they find themselves.

I hope to be that person for Lucy someday. Whenever she talks about him, envy creeps in, and sometimes I change the subject and start small talk. I can't allow myself to dwell too much on the fact that I'd given her up at birth to strangers.

But now ... now we need to concentrate on the immediate task at hand. The party. We have invited everyone we know: old friends, new friends, long-lost cousins, old co-workers. And with a quick count, it's a little over fifty people. And most of them RSVP'd yes.

Lucy doesn't think that's many people, and disappointment floods her face. She wants a party that people will talk about for ages. In her books, fifty people don't create enough energy for the party to be epic. But I try to explain to her: the more money we have, the smaller the circle of friends needs to be. Trust becomes another important currency in our lives.

Lucy sits back in her chair, holding a magazine in her hand. I lean forward and notice it's a catalogue for party supplies. She'd said earlier she wanted to fill the rooms and the front yard with balloons of multiple colors. The party calls for festive decorations, and shit—it better scream happiness from the outside.

"Hey, Lynn."

I twitch as she calls me by my name, and not Mom. I can't force her to call me Mom all the time. It's all new to her. And to me, I guess. We have to go easy on each other as we slide into each other's lives. I should be happy she's been in my constant presence since our reunion. "Should we get paper plates?" She looks at me and crunches up her nose.

I wave my hand and say, "Whatever you think is best."

She stares at me. "Okay."

"I mean, you seem keen on deciding on your own. Or with Barbara. So, go ahead."

My demeanor is bitterer than I'd intended. I get up and head for my bedroom, leaving Lucy sitting in the kitchen to pore over the catalogue. I feel her eyes boring into my back as I quickly ascend the stairs to the second floor. When I come to the landing, I take a quick look and notice Lucy staring at me. I divert my gaze and pretend I didn't see it, but I know her eyes are following me.

I wonder what she's thinking. I've gone too far with my reaction, but hopefully she won't make a fuss about it.

It pains me that I don't know my daughter that well at all. I mean, yes, on the outside, she is polite, smart, considerate, but I don't know what would set her off. How would she react if the world went to shit? Could I trust her? Would she run for the hills when all hell broke loose?

I still have to remember she is my daughter, and I need to be patient. Her living with me is a trial period and a perfect opportunity to get to know her.

But, of course, I've been a walking mess lately. The party's making me nervous. People will wonder where Jimmy is. Why wouldn't he be at the party? Well, by now, the entire town should know that Jimmy was acting like a violent asshole during our marriage, and it would be no surprise for anyone to hear we're settling a divorce. Irreconcilable differences and all that. I'm sticking to this story. As to his whereabouts? How should I know? Or care?

Life should go splendidly from now on. I will enjoy my new home. Embrace my new daughter.

And keep my secret till my grave.

LYNN SEEMS FLUSTERED these past few days. She's snappy and jumpy, taking offense to everything I say. I don't know if her behavior has something to do with her attempt to adjust to her life as a new mother or if planning for the party is too overwhelming. I wouldn't rule out either possibility.

I'm grateful she's letting me live in her new mansion. My room overlooks the ocean, and most of the time feel like I'm in a dream. After I dropped out of college, I could only find jobs that didn't pay well, so I couldn't afford anything except a box in a house shared by others. My previous roommates minded their own business, which made me lonelier. While all my friends graduated from college and moved on to get a kick-ass job, I got left behind to scramble and do the best I could. It wasn't much. But I was too ashamed to rely on my dad too much.

This is a tremendous step up from my previous digs.

Though, honestly, I wasn't entirely sure if living with

my biological mom, whom I just met after twenty-five years, was a good idea. It's like when you meet a potential partner online, and then you decide to marry a month later. At least that's how it feels. Somewhat quick and premature. I'm used to being alone, endlessly roaming the paths of New Hampshire, finding something to do. In my shitty room with a single mattress and a TV stand sitting on the floor, I'd spent hours upon hours playing video games till the wee hours, skip the morning, and start my day at noon. I was trapped in a toxic and unhealthy situation, unable to break free.

And when you spend too much time alone, your perspective on the world can shift, and your reasoning skews. So, I did my best to keep in touch with my college friends and talk to them as often as I could. Eventually, they were all too busy to pick up the phone, as they were immersed with bigger and more important things in life.

Clearly, I wasn't.

But I shouldn't worry too much about living with Lynn. The house is so big. I could easily find a way to avoid running into her. If she's lounging by the pool, I can cook in the kitchen. If she's watering the plants in the front yard, I can watch TV in the family room. Like now, for example. She went to her bedroom and God knows when I'm going to see her again.

I focus on the catalogue and look through the items to buy. I haven't planned for many parties before, only during my college days when they turned into crazy, drunken affairs, but I think I have a good sense of what we need.

I've never planned a party for over thirty people. I'm excited to meet Lynn's friends and family members. Because her relatives are also mine, by blood. I'm curious to know what relationships I could have nourished but missed all these years.

I walk to the living room and grab my computer from the coffee table. I don't remember who we invited, so I open the invite to see who has RSVP'd. These electronic invites are fabulous. Lynn wanted to be old-fashioned at first and send physical copies in the regular mail, but I talked her out of it. "Mom, nobody does that anymore unless it's a wedding or something. And nowadays some people send invitations to their wedding via email. It's the new etiquette."

She widened her eyes at me as I tried to explain how the world worked. It was like she'd just arrived from the ice age. But I guess we're two generations apart. I don't blame her if she's ignorant about these things.

The list is manageable. There are many names I don't know or recognize, but soon enough, they won't be just the names on the screen. They will be part of my life, and we will get to know each other better, create a synchronized world of close-knit relationships. A smile crawls across my face and my heart beats a little faster.

When I get to Jimmy's name, I stop to see if he has responded.

No. Nothing.

I click on his name, and it appears he didn't even open the invitation.

"Oh." I collapse into the chair and sigh. Why hadn't he opened it? Had he even seen it? Lynn has told me they are on the cusp of getting a divorce, but still. Regardless of the status of their relationship, I'm his biological daughter. Wouldn't he be curious to know me better now that he might not have a choice?

I want to get to know him, if he allows me.

Well, it's not like he didn't know I knew about him. He did. When I was a teenager, still forming opinions on what a life should be, I'd overhead the conversation my adopted parents were having about Jimmy in the kitchen. They didn't know I was standing in the corner, absorbing every word they were saying, shock and disbelief coursing through my veins at the mention of his name. In their eyes, mentioning Jimmy was their worst mistake, but they couldn't take their words back. The cat was out of the bag.

A short few months later, we lost Mary to a heart attack. It was a painful loss that begged a reevaluation of my life choices. Maybe her death is what drove me to seek out Jimmy.

I found him and asked him that we meet. He obliged. I was eighteen years old when Jimmy and I met at a McDonald in a small New Hampshire town. Fred wasn't sure it was a good idea and kept asking me if meeting Jimmy was something I wanted to do.

"Yes, I want to meet him," I'd tell Fred, even though fear was coursing through my body, and I didn't know what to expect.

On the day we agreed to meet up, Fred and I woke up

early and got ready. As we sat in the kitchen and ate our breakfast, Fred watched me intently and nervously sipped his coffee every few seconds, even though it hadn't properly cooled off. He must have been pondering what my meeting with Jimmy would bring into our lives: Confusion? Happiness? Hurt? But no one could be sure until I met him.

Before we left the house, he gave me a big hug and looked at me with his big brown eyes. I knew what he was thinking. But just because Mary, my adopted mother, had just died, it didn't mean he would lose me, too. But I told him nothing would change. I was doing this, because I was curious, like when you're dying to open a wrapped box and see what the gift is inside. Fred was more concerned that the "gift" wouldn't be what I'd expected or imagined.

We drove to the meeting place and Fred stayed in the car, waiting to be my emotional and moral support later if things didn't go as expected. I got out of his car and slowly walked into McDonald's, my nerves rattling as I looked for Jimmy. He spotted me first. He was sitting in a corner, his hand waving in the air, signaling me to come. I smiled when our eyes met, but his face remained sour.

Jimmy was cold. Gosh, I will never forget those stitched eyebrows and tight lips when he saw me. He gave me a limp hug and asked me what I wanted to eat. He didn't wait for me to answer, but suggested items he thought I might like: A Big Mac? Fries? Big soda with that? I said yes to all of it because I didn't want Jimmy to think I was being difficult. Things were already looking awkward.

We were sitting across from each other at the table and gnawing at our food. I wasn't particularly hungry, or maybe I was just too nervous, so I ate a few fries before dunking them into the sea of ketchup I'd poured onto my plate.

"You look like your mother." He chewed his food with his mouth open.

Back then, we all believed Lynn was dead. Everyone had told me that my biological mother passed at birth, and I never considered challenging those beliefs. In our very first rendezvous, Jimmy didn't mention Lynn outside of me looking like her, and it was as if she didn't exist. That sealed my belief that she probably was dead. He'd probably moved on, a faint memory of Lynn crossing his mind occasionally. All I knew was that Jimmy was married, but not to a woman I'd call my mother.

What would I know, anyway? I was too young, already molded into a person I was. Raised by a modest couple who couldn't conceive and who always treated me as their own. A couple who loved me and gave me everything I needed.

I stared at Jimmy the whole time. He mesmerized me. A sliver of guilt seeped in when I thought perhaps I was betraying my adopted father by introducing Dad no. 2, who might soon become Dad no. 1. But Jimmy helped make my guilt go away.

"Listen." Jimmy wiped his mouth with a napkin after he'd finished his meal. "I'm happy we met, but I don't want you to keep your hopes up here."

He clicked his tongue while his eyes bored into mine. My shoulders sagged, and I felt like a storm was passing through my body. I tried to settle down as I absorbed his message.

"I mean, this is all nice and fun, but I don't have time for these get-togethers. Okay? If you want us to be acquaintances, that's cool, but I won't be your dad. You already have a dad who raised you. You don't need two."

With sad eyes, I nodded and managed a small smile to abate the amount of shock Jimmy unleashed on me.

"Okay." I put my head down. There was nothing more to say. No reason to compromise, negotiate, or argue. Just because he was my biological father, it didn't mean we would form an inseparable parent/child bond.

But a small part of me did hope I'd run into him or meet up with him again. And when I didn't, mainly because he refused every time, I'd go visit his workplace or his house and watch his moves from a discrete distance. When I visited his house, the sight of him leaving made my stomach jitter and my palms sweat. I didn't have the courage to approach him, and even if I did, I knew it wouldn't go well. I'd seen the woman he lived with from afar and didn't bother to learn about her, or to question who she was. My father was my only target of interest. I became obsessed. The more I learned about him, the more he was becoming an enigma, and I wanted to find out more and more.

Over time, I created a mental checklist of things to

learn about Dad. I've always been curious about what makes him tick and what kind of lifestyle he has settled for.

No children living in the house? Check.

Married? Check.

Happy marriage? Debatable and still under close surveillance.

No pets? Check.

No friends? Check.

No happiness in life? Well, every time I saw him, his face morphed into anger or anguish. So, check.

Working my way through the checklist drew me a little closer to him. As his acquaintance, maybe I could help him get out of his life slump, find the happiness he might be struggling to reach.

Even now, all this time later, my expectations are low. No one can replace Fred, my adopted father, who has been nothing but loving and kind towards me. But a part of me is curious to know what makes up my genetic code, and what both my actual parents are like. I'm on the quest to find out more about Mom. She hasn't been keen on me inviting Jimmy to the party initially. When I made the request, I acknowledged how difficult it might be for her to be in the presence of a man who will soon be her ex, but then she caved.

"Go ahead, invite him. What do I care?" she said.

She gave me his email address, no questions asked. I'd been thrilled. One step closer to connecting to Jimmy. And I appreciated how receptive to the idea Lynn was.

There's only one way to find out what's happening with Jimmy, and why he hasn't RSVP'd.

I move the chair from behind me and head upstairs. When I get there, I gently rap my knuckles on Lynn's bedroom door.

"Yes?" I hear Lynn's voice, quiet but firm. Did I wake her up?

"Mom, can I come in?"

"Sure."

I open the door, and, on the other side, I find Lynn lying in her bed, staring at the ceiling. The air is heavy, and the room smells like death. She has an odd habit of keeping her windows closed all the time, with little interest in getting some fresh air in. I scrunch up my nose as I walk in, abating the foul smell.

"Is everything okay?" I ask.

She moves her head to the side and looks at me. "Yeah, why wouldn't it be?"

I shrug. I trot to her bed and sit on the edge, putting my hand on hers. "Hey, Mom. I need to ask you to do me a favor."

She slides her hand away from mine, as if she doesn't want me to touch her. If she were Mary, she would be reciprocating my touch, maybe even giving me a strong hug. But not Lynn. And it stings.

The atmosphere in the room tenses as Lynn widens her eyes at me. "What is it?"

"Well, I know you and Dad ... Jimmy ... are not on good terms, but I'm wondering if you'd be willing to share his phone number with me?" I play with my hands out of nervousness. "He hasn't opened my invite yet, and I'd love to know if he's coming to the party."

Lynn's eyes glaze over for a second. Her mouth opens, but no words come out. She turns her head to the other side, her eyes settling on the window, and she stares at it like that for a good while.

"Mom?"

She turns to me and says, "Um. Sure, I can do that. Let me first find my phone and I'll find you downstairs. Okay?"

She jumps out of bed before running into the bathroom next to the bedroom. The door behind her slams, then water runs in the sink. My brow furrows as I shuffle off the edge of the bed. Why the sudden departure?

I must have broached a sensitive subject for Mom. After everything she's been through as of late, this divorce is probably a hell of an emotional ride for her.

THE BATHROOM SPINS around me as I hyperventilate and hold my chest, trying desperately to catch a breath. The bedroom door shuts. Lucy's gone, filling me with relief. What will she be thinking of my reaction? I sure as shit didn't see that question coming. First, she wanted his email address, then his phone number. What's next? She'll ask him to move in. Though she won't get much of a reply.

I'm doing my darndest to keep it cool in front of Lucy, I really am, but every mention of Jimmy takes me for a whirlwind. I bend down to the sink and wash my face, hoping the cold water will bring a fresh perspective and calm me down. Seeing my new huge jacuzzi tub with jets gives me the sudden idea to fill it with hot water for a bath. I don't remember the last time I took a peaceful bath. My last place had a standing shower, just big enough for one average person to fit in.

I turn the water on, carefully adjusting for hot and cold, and take my clothes off. When the tub is sufficiently filled, I step inside and immediately feel a sense of comfort and calmness. I sit down and let the jets massage my body. Ahhh, it's so relaxing. I should take advantage of this new, fancy house, flip my life inside out like a juicy burger and swallow it whole.

Now that I have money, I've finally been able to see a doctor without worrying about how I'm going to pay my bills. Since my body was starting to fall apart, after Jimmy's unfortunate demise, I'd wanted to check in with the doctor and find out what I could do in the last days of my life. My old doctor was no longer around—he'd retired—so I found a new one, just around the corner from Red Urchin.

Going to the doctor to talk about my last few days in this world had made my heart feel heavy. I was scared and sad, thinking about what might happen. The realization of departing from Lucy so soon after being reunited was painful. Having her by my side those few days had been difficult, but easier than being alone. I knew she cared about me, and that made me feel a bit better. Even though it was tough, I wanted to face it with bravery and love. Lucy offered to come with me that day, but I told her there was no need.

Guess what?

It wasn't lung cancer. Shock had shook every bone of my exhausted body to its core. How could the last doctor have got it so wrong? Did he mix up the records and take someone else's instead of mine?

And I'd been so incredibly ill. The only explanation could have been that I was dying.

Sitting in the doctor's office that day was one of the most surreal experiences of my life. Processing the information my new doctor had given me felt impossible.

I had questions.

"How do you explain all the blood clots I was coughing out, doctor?" I asked.

"My guess is you had a severe case of pneumonia. Coughing out blood clots is one symptom."

My brows raised in surprise. "Pneumonia? Are you sure I don't have lung cancer?"

"I'm positive." She smiled. She placed the X-rays on the lit-up screen to show the scars on my lungs caused by the infection. "Your case looks to have been severe, but your recovery looks promising."

I managed to nod slowly, my head still spinning. "I was pretty sure I was in the last stages of cancer, and my old doctor told me so."

She cocked her head to the side and said, "I'm so sorry. But we doctors are human, too, and make mistakes all the time. I'm glad you came back for more tests. You should continue resting at home until you fully recover. You have still suffered a serious illness, and the body needs time to heal."

But I still had more questions for her. Like, what was all that talk about cancer spreading to my bones? Why did I feel like a walking skeleton about to collapse any minute? I felt the pain. I was confident my bones were giving up on me.

The doctor shook her head. My question stumped her.

"I... I honestly don't know. I encourage you to look further into that and see an orthopedic doctor."

As lay in the bath reflecting on the day I found out I wasn't dying after all, a thought occurs to me. Bone pain? It must be caused by all the beatings Jimmy unleashed on me. It was like he was a boxer, and I was his punching bag. And then there was the car accident that Jimmy had skillfully planned which had almost led me to my death. It all must have taken a toll on me.

As I remember those experiences, my jaw tightens and my eyes well up with tears. I don't know what I'm feeling right now: anger, self-pity, remorse ... one thing I don't feel is guilt.

I have my daughter back. She's my new life. When I first saw Lucy and realized I hadn't killed my child as I'd been led to believe, relief washed over me. Decades of accumulated shame and disgrace shaved off and melted away. Not entirely, of course. I still feel a pang of guilt for giving her up when I was at my weakest. I've lost twenty-five years living a life without my daughter. But I can make up for it.

I will make her happy and treat her like a princess.

I've been so lost in my thoughts I hadn't even realized the water has cooled down. I step outside the tub and grab the closest towel, which is a few steps away. Wow, I actually have to walk to get to a towel? I mean, this bathroom is so large, I could fit ten Jacuzzi tubs in here.

An involuntary burst laughter comes out of me. It's

filled with happiness. I'm on top of the world. I'm getting used to this new, lavish lifestyle.

No one and nothing can take it away from me.

I dry myself off and put on a pair of jeans and a shirt and head downstairs to find Lucy. Where is she? The house is so big it takes minutes for me to find her. I first look in the kitchen; she's not there. I stop to check for sounds that might reveal her whereabouts, but there's nothing. The house is eerily quiet. Lucy tends to play her metal music loudly, filling the silence, but she hasn't done that all day. I go upstairs and knock on the door of her bedroom. No answer.

Off I go downstairs again to look for Lucy. I walk through the family room and step for a second to admire its high ceilings and the intricate crown molding edging the room. I spin around twice with my spread arms and take a deep breath. The inviting smell of cinnamon wafting through the air reminds me of my childhood when we gathered at Grandma's for Christmas. Lucy was cooking earlier. She'd made her favorite blueberry cinnamon muffins.

A smile forms on my face and I pinch myself once to ensure I'm not dreaming. I'm not. It's all too real.

I peer through the window in the living room and spot Lucy lying in a chair by the pool. With her eyes closed, she's catching the mid-summer sun's rays. She's wearing a bikini top and a tight miniskirt, revealing her long, skinny legs. Her hair overflows on the back of the chair, looking like a gentle blanket. I wonder if she's sleeping. Just as the thought crosses my mind, Lucy raises her head and looks far ahead, her eyes resting on the ocean, its view extending far. Just on the edge of our property, there's a steep cliff that quickly descends into the ocean. I've feared it might become a hazard at night, but the short hedges protect access to it. I guess you can't just walk off the cliff easily without bumping into the hedge first.

Lucy is now sitting up in the chair and wipes the sweat off her forehead. I walk through the kitchen French door and descend the steps until I arrive by the pool.

Lucy sees me and gives me a smile. "Hi."

"Hi, sweetie." I cock my head to the side as I watch Lucy squint her eyes to fight off the sun's brightness. "Be careful with the sun. You can burn easily."

Lucy has a fair skin complexion, something she got from me. Not from Jimmy. He tanned so easily. It took only one tanning session in the sun for his skin tone to brown and glow. I'm more of a half-Irish pale gal who burns like a matchstick with the first sun exposure.

I feel a little odd giving Lucy unsolicited advice. I'm her mother, but we still haven't fully built mutual trust. She doesn't seem to mind. In fact, she's seems receptive to it and looks to be considering my words. She says, "Yeah, that's a good point. I really should sit in the shade. Or put a bunch of 45 SPF."

She gets up from the chair and before she walks by, she gives me a kiss on the cheek. I need to talk to her before she leaves to go back inside.

"Hey, listen," I say.

Lucy stops in her tracks and turns around to look at me. She pulls a strange face, but I'm not quite sure what it is. A grimace?

I extend my arm toward her with a piece of paper in my hand. "Here."

She looks down at my hand, wondering what I have for her. "What is it?"

"It's Jimmy's phone number. Just because we're getting a divorce doesn't mean you shouldn't be in touch with him or invite him to the party."

She walks down the stairs and takes the folded piece of paper out of my hand. "Thanks, Mom. You're a doll."

She turns around and continues walking to the house. I wonder how she'll feel when Jimmy doesn't respond. I need to find a way to shield her from negative emotions.

CHAPTER 6
LUCY

LYNN STAYS OUTSIDE to walk around and admire her new yard. It's so grand that it feels like a secret garden. Lush green grass stretches out, inviting us to kick off our shoes and feel the earth beneath our feet. Vibrant flowers bloom along the edges, dancing in the breeze as a strong oak tree in the far corner provides a comforting shade.

The backyard is even more impressive.

It's a magical oasis, centered around a sparkling swimming pool that shimmers in the sunlight. Lush, emerald-green hedges surround the area, providing a sense of privacy and tranquility. Lounge chairs beckon beside the pool, inviting relaxation and lazy afternoons under the warm sun. I don't know how to swim, but I can still dip my toes in the pool.

There's so much to appreciate: the breathtaking views, the vibrant garden, the flawless perfection of the house... so much.

This house looks nothing like the home I grew up in.

My adopted parents lived modestly, in a three-bedroom colonial, large enough for the three of us. Even at a young age, I had my own room tucked in a corner, across from my parents' bedroom. When I was young, my parents allowed me to express myself by decorating my room as I pleased. I covered the walls with posters of my favorite singers, placed trinkets from our travels on the shelves, and kept my books and diary within reach.

The enormity of this house can't compare to the house I grew up in, but I'm yet to call it a home filled with love and warmth. Plus, if I'm being frank, Lynn has been kind enough, but not warm and fuzzy like Mary was. I'm used to being showered with affection, but Lynn has a different style of showing love. There are moments when her demeanor turns chilly, like a distant breeze that briefly freezes our connection.

This is the second reason I want to get in touch with Jimmy. I'm still hoping he will come around.

Clutching the piece of paper with Jimmy's phone number, afraid to smear it with my clammy hands, I walk inside. The heat's a bit too much today, and it makes me sweat like a pig. The house feels cool with the AC on. I can't believe I'd dozed off outside. The sun nearly burned my skin, and blisters will soon emerge all over my body. When I get upstairs, I go to my bathroom and look for the aloe vera. I've heard it has great healing properties for the skin. I come across it in the drawer under the sink and slather it all over my body. I can't look like shit at the party.

Thank goodness we still have two weeks to prepare.

I've always dreamed of having a party in a fancy place, like those in Hollywood movies. But now it's a reality, and I'm the one planning for it. I wonder what it would be like to meet Jimmy again. What would I want from such an encounter? I picture our reunion with a complex mix of emotions—I'd seek understanding of his past actions, while cautiously hoping for reconciliation. Within my imagination, words float like a serene river, connecting the fragments of our relationship. But the reality remains uncertain, and I force myself to stay curious and hopeful.

We wouldn't need to see each other often. I'd never demand an unreasonable amount of time with Jimmy. I'd like to just be able to call him occasionally and have a little chat. It doesn't take much effort for this to happen.

As I review the invitation responses, I'm relieved that almost all the people on my side are coming. I'm excited to show them where I live. Who my mom is. The fact that I have a mom. When word spread around that she was alive, everyone was excited for me. At first, they didn't know what to say, but then most messages turned congratulatory, with hugs and kisses and hearts accompanying the texts. It's a good feeling.

And now I'm just a phone call away closer to Jimmy. I sit down on my bed and unfold the piece of paper that Lynn gave me. Ah yes, the familiar NH area code 603. I grab my phone, ready to dial, but my heart pounds hard. I can feel the pulse in my neck. I fear he will just hang up on me when he realizes I'm the one calling him. The daughter he abandoned, the child he didn't want to have. We don't need to be close, so I'm just hoping for a cordial conversation. After all, it's just a party I'm inviting him to. We can keep it cool and casual.

I take a few deep breaths to gather my thoughts. My mind is creating a conversation, and I imagine Jimmy's reaction when he hears my voice.

"Who's this?"

"Um. Hi, it's me, Lucy."

Silence.

"What do you want?"

"Um, yeah. I sent you an invitation to the housewarming. Did you get it?"

"What invitation?"

Hm. That's why he never responded. He never saw it. Maybe my email went to his spam folder. Emails from an unknown address can do that.

"We have a party here in two weeks, and I'd love you to —" Wait, I need to tone this down. *"I'd like you to come. It'll be fun."*

"Lucy—"

Ugh! What am I doing? I should just dial the number, stop worrying, and be myself. The worst that can happen is he will hang up on me. I've experienced worse.

I put in all of his phone digits on my phone and push the call button. It's ringing. It's ringing. When the call goes to his voicemail, my butterflies turn into disappointment, and I kick myself for feeling nervous a few seconds earlier.

No response. Maybe Jimmy doesn't take calls from numbers he doesn't have programmed on his phone. Quite possible. I know a few other people who don't do it, me included. He could be busy and has his phone tucked in somewhere. Anything is possible.

But a strange feeling gnaws at me when I think of another possibility.

What if something is wrong with Jimmy? What if he might have fallen ill, lying somewhere in a hospital? Something just doesn't seem right here, and my instinct is nearly always right.

I have a suspicion that Jimmy isn't safe. After all, it's been days since I sent the party invite. I haven't met a person yet who doesn't check their email for that long.

In panic, I dial him again, but the call goes into his voicemail. It occurs to me to send him a quick text, which I guess could have been my first choice, but I wanted an immediate response. I wanted to hear his voice. I type a message and hit send. I'm rereading it over and over and over:

Hi, it's Lucy.

My hand is shaking as I'm waiting for his response. I'm staring at the phone, expecting a text back any second, praying for the three dots to appear to show he's typing, but there's nothing. I'd settle for the three dots to at least know he's okay and alive.

I don't know how long I end up staring at the phone, waiting for a sign, but as time goes by, my hope plunges, and I feel depleted.

I storm out of my room and head outside. Where the hell is Lynn?

I nearly trip and fall as I skip the steps leading to the first floor. I find Lynn standing outside, her palm balanced above her forehead to shield her from the bright sunlight, as she watches the ocean in the far distance. She hears me stomping on the ground, dashing toward her. I can see her profile before she completely turns around and faces me.

"Mom." I stare at her with scared eyes. "I think something is wrong with Jimmy."

"OH, dear. Why do you say that?"

"Well, I keep calling him constantly, but he's not responding. And he hasn't even opened the invitation yet. Don't you think something could be wrong?"

Lynn comes with her arms open wide and gives me a big hug. It doesn't last long. She moves away from me, strokes my hair, moving it to the side, and says, "Jimmy's fine. That's just how he is. He has never liked phones. Did you leave him a voice mail?"

"No." I take a deep breath. "I left him a text. He hasn't responded yet."

She waves her hand and makes a face. "Oh, don't worry. He will get back to you. But if he doesn't, it's typical Jimmy. You have to call him a million times before he responds." Lynn laughs.

"I don't understand why he's like this or why he's rejected me." My voice wobbles. I hate rejections. When I realized Lynn was my mom, I didn't approach her immediately, fearing she'd follow Jimmy's suit and want nothing to do with me. I stalked her instead. She became my new obsession, while Jimmy was no longer my main target.

Maybe she could have tried to kill me as a baby, who knows?

I'm glad this isn't the case. I wish I'd approached her sooner, but it took me a while to muster the courage.

I know I'm preaching to the choir, and Lynn may not have all the answers, but she knows him better than I ever will. She might have some answers for me.

She takes my hands. "You know what? How about we go to a salon for a manicure and pedicure? What do you say?" Her enormous eyes bore into me. "I'd love me some mom and daughter quality time."

Despite everything she's going through with Jimmy, a divorce and all, Lynn is doing her best. She tries hard to make these feelings of rejection go away, and she will do anything to make me feel better, accepted. It can't be easy for her to upend her life, reconnecting with her daughter out of the blue and losing her husband at the same time. A loss is a loss, even if it ultimately leads to relief in life.

"Let me get ready, and we can go," I tell her, with little enthusiasm in my voice.

"Cheer up," she says in a singsong voice.

"Okay." I smile.

We both trot upstairs to our respective bedrooms. They're across from each other, so sometimes I can hear Lynn singing or talking on the phone. I put on a dress and a little makeup in the bathroom and, while combing my hair, the urge to call Jimmy again overtakes me. I step outside the bathroom and take my phone from the charger. My hand is shaky, but I dial Jimmy.

In the near distance, I hear a phone ring. Must be Lynn's phone. I refocus my energy on the call and try to calm my nerves at the same time. I crane my neck toward the ceiling and close my eyes, but as soon as I realize Jimmy isn't picking up again, I open them again.

"Shit!"

Lynn startles me by knocking heavily on my door and speaking loudly. "Sweetheart, are you ready?"

Why the urgency? Surely a little pampering isn't that much of an emergency? I approach the door and open it to see Lynn standing there with a smile that doesn't quite reach her eyes.

"Sure," I say. I don't tell her I called Jimmy. She'll think I've become obsessed with his lack of acknowledgment.

Which I am.

The lingering fear of rejection has intensified, and I can't shake it off easily.

On our way to the salon, we're quiet. Lynn is driving in her new car—Toyota Acura—which is an odd choice, given her newfound wealth. It's a good car, don't get me wrong, but most people would choose to buy a BMW or a Mercedes. But she had to go with a friggin' Toyota? Maybe she hasn't mentally processed her wealth yet.

She cares for her new car well and seems to be proud of it. Since the day we moved, she's already taken it for a wash every week and had the oil changed even though we've barely driven anywhere. It warms my heart that she has the ability to care for things.

Lynn looks at me occasionally and lowers her head to see me above the rim of her sunglasses. "What was the last time you went for a mani-pedi?"

I shake my head. "Never."

My whole life, I've never been a girly girl. Whenever Fred gave me pocket money, I'd save it for tattoos. Manicures and pedicures have never been my choice of beauty treatment. Nail polish is temporary. Tattoos are permanent, and I like things to stick around a lot longer.

"Never?" She raises her voice, playfully pretending to be in shock. "Well, you're in for a treat, young lady."

When we get there, the salon is empty. One, it's in the town's periphery, where people would bother venturing only for a specific errand. And two, it's Monday morning, so almost everyone is working or surviving the first day of workweek. Not us. We're exploring ways to occupy ourselves and indulge in self-care while strengthening our bond.

Two ladies at the salon seat us next to each other so we can get a pedicure simultaneously, while we giggle and enjoy this new adventure. Inside the salon, the air is infused with the delicate scent of lavender and vanilla, creating a surreal sense of calm. I clutch the strap of my bag tightly, my heart racing, though I'm not entirely sure why. It could be about Lynn and me stepping out for the first time and the risks of running into unwanted individuals.

Lynn chooses a chair near the window and gestures for me to sit, and I oblige, settling into the chair next to her.

A young manicurist with a welcoming smile approaches us, offering a polite greeting. Her name tag reads "Lila".

"Good afternoon. What can we do for you ladies today?"

"We'd like pedicures, please. The works," Lynn says.

I shift uncomfortably in my seat, my eyes darting around the room. The sunlight filters through the curtains, casting intricate shadows across the space. A knot of unease forms in the pit of my stomach. Why did I agree to come here? I need to relax. I need to trust my mother.

"Of course, ladies. Please make yourselves comfortable. We'll start with a warm foot soak and some pampering."

Another young woman comes from around the curtain and approaches Lynn. She looks indifferent; her job done on an autopilot.

As Lila fills a basin with steaming water, my mother watches me closely. Her hazel eyes, identical to mine, are like mirrors reflecting my every emotion. I feel a sudden rush of vulnerability, as if I'm under a microscope. But I shake off the feeling and let Lila do her magic.

Out of the corner of my eye, as Lila is massaging my left foot, I see a familiar face outside the salon. He walks by, looking straight ahead, somewhat oblivious to his surroundings. As I concentrate more, I realize it's Evan.

What the hell is he doing here? I mean, yes, the town is small, and you could easily run into a person you know, but

I'd never in a million years expect to see Evan here. It's Monday morning, and he should be at work.

I flinch at the image of him that falls into my mind, and my cheeks flush with heat. I twist and cover the side of my head with my hand as if shielding myself from the outside.

I can't tell Lynn about Evan. For many reasons. First, he's about Lynn's age, four or five years younger than her, and a lot older than me. Like, twice. But if you saw him, you'd never guess he was fifty. He looks young for his age, energetic, and he likes to hang out with younger folks, like me.

And second, what would she think her daughter was doing wasting her time away with a man twice her age? Only Rebecca, my college friend, knows my secret. I don't want to be judged for the choices I've made. I want Lynn to think I'm following a path of any other average young woman. Fall in love with someone my age, get married, and then build a family.

But with Evan? All of that is a certain impossibility.

We hang out, usually at his place, watching movies, smoking weed. That's all we do. Smoking weed has become my pastime, a habit from my college years. The apple doesn't fall far from the tree, as they say, or maybe it's the fact that when Lynn used drugs during her pregnancy, it entered her bloodstream and went right into me. Weed is as far as I'd go. Though, it's become a habit I can't kick so easily. When Evan and I get together, that's what we do. We smoke, we have sex, we tell ourselves this relationship is of mutual convenience. I get my weed; he gets his sex.

Three months into our affair, he gave me keys to his place so I can come and go as I wish. I took them because his place became my refuge, a comfortable place I could crash and relax.

Thankfully, the mysterious image I saw through the glass is gone now. When I remove my hand, I notice Lynn staring at me. "Everything okay?"

"Yes." I divert my gaze from her and check out Lila, who's working on my toes. I turn to Lynn to break the news. "I've been meaning to tell you this earlier, but I don't want to wait anymore."

Her brows raise. "What is it?"

"I'm looking for a job, something easy to spend my time on. Maybe some volunteer work." I take my T-shirt and pull it against my body, a common nervous action of mine.

She studies me after I tell her my news.

When Lynn and I reunited, she told me I didn't have to worry about my living expenses or finding a job. At my last job as a front desk receptionist at a real estate agency, my boss fired me, because I was consistently late to the office. Not just a few minutes, but sometimes as long as an hour. I used to get so absorbed in my morning routine that I'd forget I had to leave by a specific time to be punctual at work. He got fed up and told me one day never to return. I've looked for a job sporadically but have had little luck in this tough economy.

I've been lucky to live with Lynn.

She'd pay for everything, she told me. With a million

and a half in her savings account, she has been getting a hefty interest payment every month, the amount high enough to live from. The only reason she's let me leach off her for now is to allow us to spend time together. While we can't make up all the time we've lost, we can at least enjoy each other's company for as long as we can.

Lynn looks distraught, her eyes etched in surprise. "Oh," she says. "Okay. I didn't realize you were looking for a job."

"Just a part-time gig, so I can get out of the house and be out of your hair for a little while." I smile at her to subdue the awkwardness.

I have convinced her of my intentions, but she doesn't know the truth. Nor will she find out.

Her face finally cracks into a smile. "I'm so proud of you, darling. I'm sure your efforts will pay off."

PARENTING IS SO HARD. Who knew? Couple that with hating surprises, I feel totally blindsided by the news Lucy delivered. No matter how much I disapprove of her decision to get a job or volunteer somewhere, I'm going to support her. I have to. I don't want to appear a control freak, questioning every decision or move she makes.

She's fidgeting in her seat, looking nervous and uncomfortable. What's going on? I watch her shield her face from something outside, but I can't tell what it is. Whatever it may be, it's already gone. Her eyes keep gazing at the window, as if she's expecting for whatever object she fears to appear again.

"Everything okay?" I ask her again.

"Yeah." She nods. "Actually, do you mind if we skip the manicures? I'm not feeling well."

"Oh. What's wrong?"

"I'm just feeling a little dizzy."

Did I say parenting was hard? I'll say it again because

it so darn is. I'm new to it, but I can already see how much a parent needs to sacrifice to ensure happiness for their child. I'm trying hard to please Lucy and do some fun activities with her, but she seems troubled about something, yet she doesn't want to share what it is with me. It's so frustrating. But I know it all goes back to building trust between us. We're not there yet, I get it. For now, I appease her, so she can see me as a mother she can rely on and turn to during tough times.

"I'm sorry, sweetie. No problem." I look down at our feet and watch the ladies painting our toenails. "Looks like we're almost done here."

In the car, on our way home, Lucy has completely changed her disposition. She raises her feet on the dashboard, leans low on her seat, and opens the side window. Her elbow hangs out, her hair fluttering like a flag in the wind. She doesn't look sick or perturbed. She's humming to the music blasting through the speakers and tapping her feet against the dashboard.

"Mind if I turn the music down?" I yell for attention.

She's into metal, which I rarely mind, but a headache is creeping up, and I'd prefer peace right now.

She reaches for the volume dial and turns the music down a little. It's still too loud for my taste, but I say nothing. I suck it up and remain focused on the road.

When commercials replace music on the radio, I turn it all the way down and I ask her if she wants to go somewhere and have lunch. On a day like this, we can find a restaurant along the beach with an outside seating and watch people walk by as we absorb the sun.

She's not even looking at me as she responds, "Nah. Let's just go home."

"Okay."

My shoulders slump as discouragement takes hold of me. I don't know what's going on with Lucy, and she doesn't want to tell me. As we pull over in our driveway, I push the gear into park and turn to face Lucy, who's surveying her fingernails. "You know, I wish we'd done the manicure, too. I don't know why you rushed us to leave."

My jaw drops to the floor. "I ... I thought you weren't feeling well, so we left."

She's reaching for the door to open it and says as nonchalant as possible, "But I'm okay now. You didn't have to panic so much."

With that, she exits the car and heads for the front door. I unbuckle my seat belt and rush to follow Lucy, but she's already gone through the front door and up the stairs to her bedroom. Should I follow her? Against my better judgment, I stomp across the living room and rush up the stairs to meet Lucy in her room. I knock on her door and patiently wait for her to open the door. Nothing. I knock on the door again and her voice on the other side projects loudly, "I'm taking a nap. Can you leave me alone?"

My body sags, and a rush of anxiety flows through me. It seems like she's avoiding me, and I don't know what I've done to deserve it. I tell her, "Okay," and turn around, devising the ways which could bring us closer. The more I think, the more panic strikes me. I don't know if I even ever could trust Lucy, despite our brief history, and she's the closest living being to me right now.

I must keep her on my side even though, in spirit and soul, we're as far from each other as distant galaxies.

I'M STILL REELING from seeing Evan earlier. Was he following me again?

I step into the bathroom to take a shower. I could call Evan to find out what he was doing in that neighborhood, but I'd rather go to his place, unannounced, and ask him in person. Of course, it could entirely be coincidental that he was at the same time and place as me and Lynn, but he'd also found me having dinner with a friend at a local restaurant one time, and he showed up at my workplace unannounced on another occasion.

All these coincidences make me wonder if Evan wants more than a casual relationship. These regular occurrences of running into him give me strange vibes.

But I've told Evan it will never happen between us. I can count on one hand the number of times I've fallen for a guy, and every time, it was a disaster. They all told me they weren't ready for a serious relationship, and the rejection broke my heart every time. There was something about me that repelled them, something that convinced them I'm not the one and never will be.

Sure, I've gone to a therapist who told me I had abandonment issues, given Jimmy's outright rejection. And sure, I had Fred, who loves and cares about me, but I couldn't help but take the rejection personally. It cut deep, slashing every ounce of confidence I had. There's no way in hell my chances of connecting with another being would happen soon. Evan can only dream about it.

Besides, he should know better, given our age difference. I'm more like an injured bird caught outside and put in a cage, but I will be set free whenever I recover.

Later that day, I finally leave my room and find Lynn sitting cross-legged on the couch in the living room with her eyes closed. When she hears my steps, she peels her eyes open and looks at me.

"I'm going to run an errand," I say. "I should be back in a few."

"Oh, okay." Her voice is soft, full of hesitation. "Do you want us to cook dinner when you get back? Together? Something simple, like pasta maybe."

"Sure."

She tilts her head and playfully says, "I can boil water for pasta if you want me to. I can help."

I'm fully aware of Lynn's cooking skills. She burns water, for crying out loud, so I will probably end up doing that as well.

I pull my phone out of my pocket and see it's around four. "I should be back by six or seven at the latest."

"Okay. Well, be careful out there and have fun whatever you're doing."

I approach Lynn and give her a kiss on the cheek. She doesn't kiss me back. Part of me feels bad for acting like a jerk earlier. Maybe I don't deserve a kiss from Lynn right now. But any surprise encounter with Evan makes me nervous. There's no way in hell I'd want to tell Lynn about him. Just because I have these fears of attachment and I'm worried about her finding out that I'm seeing a much older guy, doesn't mean I should mistreat her.

I enter the three-car garage and get into the blue Mustang I've had for several years. Fred helped me pay for it. God bless his generous soul. I sit in the car, turn on the engine, and listen to it roar, as the sound awakens all my senses. I pull out of the garage and head for the road I've taken so many times before.

Evan's place is a fifteen-minute ride from my new home. I'm picturing a scene when I get there and take deep breaths as I prepare to deliver my speech. I feel a knot in my stomach, a burning feeling to tell him off, but staying calm will serve me better, so I take another deep breath.

When I arrive at his place, I don't see his car in front. He lives in a single-family house, all alone. The house is secluded, with few neighbors around. I've wondered why he needs a big house, and how he could afford to live alone, but I never crossed that line with Evan. It's his business, so I don't want to pry. He asked me once if I wanted to move in, given the size of his house, but I refused. I didn't want to mislead him into believing that it meant something.

I get out of the car and approach the front door, which is ajar. Did Evan leave his house unlocked? This is so unlike him. He must be distracted today. Something must be happening.

One step in front of the other, I inch forward, afraid someone might be waiting on the other side. When the door is completely open, I yell out, "Hello?" I say it loud enough for my voice to project through the house, but there's no response. I sigh in relief and proceed inside, taking my sunglasses off and putting my purse on the couch. Right away, I shoot for the kitchen and find myself a refreshing drink in the fridge. It's super-hot outside, with no wind to cool off the air.

While waiting for Evan to come home, I help myself to things, as usual. I turn the TV on and sit on the couch, placing my feet on the coffee table. We've had sex on this couch so many times, and when I am all alone at his place, that's the only association I have with his furniture.

As I watch the TV, my eyes drift toward the photos on the TV stand. A young boy with sad eyes is staring at the camera, attempting a smile. Evan told me he was his son, and he was five in that picture, but he didn't want to divulge any more. He only told me he hasn't seen his son since, and I wonder if this is the last photo Evan took of him.

The door opens and I snap out of my thoughts. I turn around and see Evan closing the front door. When he sees me, a genuine smile lights up his face, even though his eyebrows are stitched together.

"Well, hello, lady. Fancy seeing you here!" He comes to me and plants a kiss on top of my head. He is gentle and kind and doesn't know what I'm about to unleash upon him.

I'M BORED. I wish Lucy wouldn't leave the house like this and be gone for hours at a time. I wonder where she goes and whether she sees anyone. She never tells me. I could ask, but I don't want to appear nosy. I've always valued privacy.

To kill time, I mediate. Meditation has been good for me, but one can do only so much of it. Meditation is also what I've chosen over drugs. It's worked mostly well so far, but when I meditate, my mind wanders, and I can no longer stay in the present. The thoughts of my past return, and I can't help but think about Jimmy. When I stand in my backyard, I can see the ocean where Skull and his partner disposed of him. It makes me sick to think of his dismembered body.

Maybe I need to reconnect with my friends and hang out with them more often. I've invited Greta and Barbara to our party, and I hope this is a chance to rekindle our connection. The only person close to me I haven't invited is Skull. Truth be told, I feel guilty about it, but since he is so close to Jimmy's death, I can't risk his appearance. What if he blurts out what I did in front of everyone (although, quite unlikely)? What if someone asks about Jimmy in his presence, and he fidgets, showing something funky has gone down?

The risk is too high. I can't have him around. But I do need to prepare for everyone's inquisition about my life: my newfound motherhood, Jimmy's disappearance, my new home. It's like I've been handed a new life, and everyone wants to jump in on it.

As I reflect on what life has become, I realize boredom is my enemy. My biggest problem. I don't have a job to go to, and no reason for one. I can live comfortably with the lottery money until I die. I don't have any hobbies either. Nothing to occupy my mind and soul with. This is what my life with Jimmy amounted to: a fucking waste of time.

Boredom can wrack havoc on your mind, and lead to the unimaginable. I do my best to curtail the urge to become the careless person I used to be and think of things to do. Watching TV is the only thing that comes to mind, so I put it on and find a random movie. The acting in this indie horror film is just awful. I switch to a rom-com, which better suits my mind.

But I can't sit still. I fidget on the couch and have a hard time paying attention to the movie. I stand up and head to my room. When I get there, I open the side table drawer and locate the phone I've been holding onto in secrecy.

Jimmy's phone.

I've kept it around to see if Anna, his extramarital partner and mother of their child, Emma, keeps pursuing him. Since that last time I found her messages, she has called only twice, and then she stopped. My guess is her lawyer will send a follow-up letter soon. It will end up unopened and wasted, since we no longer live in the small row house.

I don't have Jimmy's phone password. But I can see all the missed messages and calls piled up on the phone. One of them is Lucy's. I can't believe I didn't have it on silent when Lucy called him the other day. I'm an idiot. That kind of carelessness will surely lead to a disaster, so I need to be more careful.

I double check the silent button is flipped down and put Jimmy's phone back in the drawer. A sudden thought comes to me like a flash. I exit my room and cross the hallway, arriving at Lucy's bedroom door, breathless. My hands shake with fear. What if I find something vile on the other side of it? But I know Lucy isn't here, and the room is empty. I nuzzle the door open and step inside. Lucy's room is a giant mess. Her clothes are scattered all over the floor; her bed is unmade; the windows are wide open, letting the summer heat in while the AC is working at a full blast. Anger runs through my veins, but fear that she might catch me in her room overrides it as soon as it comes.

I spin around and look at the mess she's made. We don't venture to each other's bedroom often, so this is the first time I've seen the evidence of Lucy's living habits. Is she always this messy? Does it reflect her mind: disorganized and tangled with problems? I don't know what exactly I'm looking for, but I approach the dresser across her bed and open each drawer, staring at the content inside. In the top drawer, all her underwear is piled up into an incomprehensible mess. I push them to the side to see if anything is hidden, but there's nothing. The second drawer stores all her T-shirts and there're dozens in all colors. My daughter dresses casually, and the long, unkempt hair gives her a look of a bum.

I open the last drawer and finally spot something that could be of interest. A small notebook with her name scribbled in the front. Should I open and explore what's inside those pages? I hesitate, unable to take my eyes away from it, and uncertain whether to open that can of worms. Because, if we're to build trust, I need to believe that Lucy isn't hiding anything questionable from me. Deep down, I have to trust that she's on my team. The powerful urge to close the drawer and forget about the snooping snaps me out of my trance.

What the hell is wrong with me? What am I doing investigating Lucy's life?

I must get out of her room. Maybe some fresh air will do me good. I stroll out of the house and walk around the grounds, hastening my steps and surveying the edges of our yard. None of our next-door neighbors have made an appearance yet, and even if they did, they'd be just silhouettes roaming around. They'd be too far away to exchange niceties and converse with. I miss Rose, my old neighbor.

As annoying as she was, I found comfort in having her around.

I look up at the sky, not seeing a single cloud. The day is gorgeous. It's such a pity to be alone on this beautiful day, but I brush the feeling aside and take a deep breath as the sun beams down on my skin. I stroll across the front yard and continue through the front gate until I land on the sidewalk. The street we live on is relatively quiet. A few cars pass by, and most of them belong to our neighbors. Some of the houses surrounding us are somebody's vacation homes, inhabited for just a few weeks in the summer, and empty the rest of the year. It's an affluent neighborhood, and I feel fortunate to be living here.

When I approach the mailbox, I see a person approaching me at the periphery of my vision. A man, maybe in his late fifties, is taking big steps toward me, and then he stops when he gets near.

"Howdy, neighbor!"

Now that he's standing in one place, I can see him a lot better. He's tall, muscular, and suntanned, and his glowing white teeth dominate his face. His blue eyes are glittering, a sign of a content person with no care in the world.

"Hi." I stand squarely in his direction, holding junk mail in my hand.

"You just moved here, right?"

"Ye ... yeah."

"Welcome to the neighborhood!" he says and extends his arm to shake my hand. I get closer and take his hand in mine, feeling his soft skin against my rough one. "I'm James."

I squirm when I hear his name and snap my hand out of his. My gaze shoots down to the ground, and I feel nervous just hearing his name. James. *Do I need another James in my life?*

He looks at me quizzically and smiles. "Aren't you going to say your name?"

"Lynn. I'm Lynn."

He squints his eyes and tilts his head, as if thinking hard. "Wait a second," he says, "I think I know you. I've seen you around."

My face goes pale, and my knees buckle under me. If anyone says they know me, I always wonder if they know more, a lot more, about me.

Like the fact that I murdered my spouse.

"Oh." That's all I say.

"You work at Red Urchin, that restaurant along the beach, don't you? I've been there quite a few times. I think I saw you there. Am I right?" He smiles, pleased with himself.

"No. No. That's not me. I don't work there."

"Are you sure? I mean, I could swear it's you."

James's face turns red and serious. It is obvious he doesn't like to be challenged and needs to be validated. But I don't have an ounce of strength to engage in this conversation or reveal anything more about myself. I'm afraid he'd only want to know more. I don't want anyone digging about me or my past. And he strikes me as someone who might do exactly that.

I take my phone out of my pocket and pretend I've received a call. "Oh, I'm sorry. I have to take this."

I give James a small wave with the hand holding the junk mail and turn with the phone resting on my ear. Pretending to talk on the phone always does the trick, even if corny. I walk across my yard, quickening my steps, and when I get halfway, I turn around and see James over my shoulder standing by the front gate of my house and watching me, his eyes a mix of puzzlement and hatred. This is a strange encounter that I hope doesn't turn even stranger.

There's no way to escape my past. But I can pretend I have left it behind.

I'M STANDING in the middle of Evan's living room, my arms resting on my hips. "What were you doing at the strip mall earlier today? Were you stalking me again?" I get right to the point.

Evan barely sits down to relax before I barrage him with questions, and he clearly doesn't appreciate it. His brows furrow. "What are you talking about? I was nowhere near the strip mall today."

He turns and heads to the kitchen to get a glass of water. After fetching a glass from the cabinet, he slams the door in annoyance. He returns to the living room, stopping in the middle and fixing me with a creased forehead. Gosh, he looks so much older when he's angry. I can't stand to look at him.

"I'm pretty sure I saw you around eleven this morning. You were wearing a baseball hat and a blue T-shirt."

I take a better look at him and notice he's neither wearing a hat nor anything blue. A black tank top shows off his well-defined muscles, which he works on so diligently. The gym is his second home, and he has a lifetime membership at one down the street from his house.

It's possible I may have mistaken him for someone else, but a feeling of unease gnaws at me. I can't help but wonder if Evan is intentionally trying to run into me or locate my whereabouts. The reason remains a mystery, but I suspect he wants reassurance that I'm not seeing other people, even though we're not in a committed relationship. Men often enjoy pursuing a challenging target, a woman who isn't easily won over. According to this definition, I'm an easy target. I'm fine with running into him when I'm alone or with a friend, but it's not acceptable when I'm with Lynn. Period.

He sits down on the couch next to me and hugs me, looking me straight in the eye.

"No, it wasn't me. And stop with the questions. You're driving me crazy now." He leans in and kisses my lips, though I don't reciprocate. "I promise you it wasn't me. I'd tell you."

I watch him in defeat and realize he's probably telling the truth. "Okay," I sigh. What is happening to me? Why was I imagining seeing Evan? Fear sometimes does that. It creates unwanted images and leads to self-fulfilling prophecy. I've got to stop.

"And you? What were you doing at the strip mall, young lady?"

"I was with my new mom." I roll my eyes and add

sarcasm to my tone. "She took me out for a mani-pedi, trying to cheer me up and all that."

Evan quickly removes his arm from my shoulder and stands up, heading to the kitchen to refill his water glass, even though it's already half full (or half empty). He always seems uncomfortable during parent-child conversations, as if an invisible hand is choking him. Initially, he showed an interest in my new mom and asked questions, but I gave him brief answers, revealing only as much as I would to a grocery store cashier. I avoid delving into my personal life with Evan.

Over time, he became silent and contemplative, likely reminded of his own parental issues. Supposedly, Evan had a child with a woman he'd dated but never married. She had commitment issues, but she liked Evan enough to stick around. Evan seems to attract commitment-phobic partners, most likely unintentionally, and breaking the cycle is challenging without understanding the core issue. Evan doesn't strike me as someone who has mastered understanding his own issues.

Evan was once thrown into despair, and he knows what it is to experience overwhelming guilt as a parent. When his son was six years old, Evan failed to buckle him in his car seat for school one morning, distracted and exhausted from his erratic work hours. That morning, he missed an important detail and didn't ensure his son's safety. The child, out of curiosity, played with the door lock, opening the car door, and fell onto a busy street, getting hit by another car. The incident left him paralyzed in both legs, forever changing his childhood. Well, life, really.

Evan's girlfriend, the child's mother, wanted nothing to do with Evan after the accident. She shielded their child from him for years, leaving Evan with only a few photos in his living room. She never gave him a second chance to redeem himself.

I avoid discussing parenthood with Evan and I downplay my relationship with Lynn to avoid reopening his wounds. There are many other things I haven't told him, like details about my biological father or our upcoming housewarming party. We usually talk about movies, food, tattoos. He has boasted about his gun collection even though he doesn't use any of them. Having a hobby, like collecting useless items, numbs some of the pain. I know why he does it, but I don't mention it or ask questions. No one makes a big deal about Evan's past, even though everyone knows about it. What he did that morning wasn't deliberate, but good luck explaining that to the child's mom.

I've sometimes wondered what would be like if things between Evan and me were serious. Would we be happy? Miserable? Would we misunderstand each other all the time, given the generational gap? It's not something I like to think about often, but these thoughts do come to mind sometimes. The least I could do is invite him to our housewarming party and introduce him as a friend.

As these thoughts linger, I shake my head. I won't invite Evan to our party. It would be a terrible idea.

THAT JAMES GUY gives me bad vibes. The minute he said he knew me from Red Urchin, I recognized him immediately. I'd seen him at the restaurant dozens of times, and I'd served him lunch and dinner. He always ordered the same thing every time: the chicken parmesan. He also preferred to sit in the same spot in a corner, if available, usually all alone. Sometimes, he'd come in casual clothes, after spending time at a beach, and other times, he'd wear his cop uniform, a gun by his side.

Red Urchin was a place that attracted cops and other interesting people you'd ordinarily never meet in a restaurant. It's almost as if Barbara owned a place to serve as a hot spot for the enforcement and bad guys alike. Sometimes, the line between the two is blurry.

That's where I met Skull. He was good friends with Barbara, and she told me he was the guy if I needed "supplies."

Just when I think I'm safe, and that no one will know me in the new neighborhood, James reemerges. I don't like it at all.

I go to my room, lock the door, and sit at my desk in the corner, frantically opening my laptop. His first name is James, but I never learned his last name. If I look him up by James only and the name of our street, my search should turn something up, right? The internet is clever these days; it finds things one would never dream of finding. I need to know where exactly he lives and whether I might run into him all the time, or whether seeing him today was a coincidence.

Or it might not be a coincidence at all.

He might be here for a reason, like to investigate my whereabouts and spy on me. I suspect he was one of Jimmy's buddies, the common thread in his life. He made friends with so many cops that, whenever he got into trouble with other people, his cop friends would let him go and not make him pay for the consequences of his misdeeds. In return, he'd be fixing their cars for free, the fancy, expensive ones they'd show off around the town and drive in like drunken teenagers. It's like a cult.

Jimmy was a player, and he knew how to play his game once he figured out how to get away with shit. But now I need to focus on the cop.

I type in JAMES and Ocean Boulevard in the internet browser. We live in the cul-de-sac, which has so few houses you could count them on two hands. It's secluded from the rest of the town, and those who live here year-round know each other well.

I push the ENTER button to get one result.

James Smith. Born July 15, 1980.

The James I encountered today can't be this young. I've seen several grays sticking out of his hair and a more than a few wrinkles hugging his nose and eyes. He strikes me as someone who just recently retired and living life to the fullest.

I expand my search by adding the profession to his name. Even so, nothing comes up. Shivers course through my spine when it occurs to me that the cop may not be living around here. His appearance on our street may not be a coincidence.

A sudden knock on the door startles me. Lucy is back home. I close the computer screen and turn around.

"Yes?"

"Hey, it's me. Can I come in?" the doorknob twists but the door doesn't open. I approach and unlock the door, finding Lucy at the doorway, staring at me with her wide eyes. "Your door is locked?"

"Oh, I didn't mean to. It's just an old habit of mine." I recount all the times I've locked myself in my bedroom to protect myself from Jimmy, who might attack me. I wouldn't dare mention it. I just wave Lucy in. "Come."

She steps inside hesitantly, looking around as if

searching for something. She gazes at the windows. "Have you considered opening the windows a little? Just to get some fresh air in?" Her nose scrunches up as if to show she doesn't like the smell in my room.

Keeping all windows and doors closed all the time is another habit of mine, but I don't want to repeat myself. Jimmy and I had an interesting way of keeping our place locked all the time, as if shielding ourselves from the outside world. Yet, what went on inside could never be shielded from each other.

"The AC is on," I tell her, hoping the excuse is good enough.

She sits on my bed, placing her hands behind her back, giving me a sad look. "I came to apologize for what happened earlier today. I was acting like a brat, and I want you to know I won't do it again."

My head snaps back in shock that she'd say anything about what transpired earlier today after we came home from the salon. I'm not used to people apologizing. My cheeks flush as I look around the room, looking for a perfect response.

I gaze at the floor as my fingers play with each other. "Thank you." I look at her shyly and give her a smile. "Thanks. That means a lot."

She stands up from the bed, clapping her hands and looking relieved her apology has been accepted. "Good. I've got a couple of things to do before the party." She waves her index finger at me and continues, "Don't forget to rest up beforehand."

I nod and smile. That won't be a problem.

If she only knew that resting is the least of my concerns.

THE DAY of our housewarming party has arrived.

The front of the house is adorned with colorful balloons, while the inside is arranged in peroration for the food, drinks, and music. I've already completed the plans: the food will arrive late morning, caterers will handle drinks and food service, and a DJ will provide the music. The back lawn is lit by Christmas lights at the edges, adding a serene atmosphere to the place. I'm excited about the party, but also nervous about how things will unfold. Will mine and Lynn's world mash well together?

I'm running through the list of invited people, and the thought of Jimmy never returning my text or call still haunts me. I've not only put a lot of thought into Jimmy's rejection, overthinking about it, ruminating all the possibilities, but sometimes, Jimmy comes to my dreams as nightmares, frowning and screaming at me, telling me to disappear.

I slide into the pantry next to the kitchen and take my

phone out. I stare at it for at least half a minute while contemplating whether to give it another try. I shake my head in dismay, in denial that Jimmy doesn't want to talk to me. Why would he? He was clear about his reasons back then, but I can't easily get over it. I can't help but take it personally.

I locate his number and push the call button. It's ringing. Five rings later, the call goes into voicemail, and there goes another unsuccessful attempt to reach him. Jimmy is a jerk. An excuse of a human being. But I will try not to think about it. I will do my best to have fun today.

When I come out of the pantry, Lynn is standing in the kitchen and staring through the window at the ocean. She sees me and jumps. "Oh, here you are. I've been looking for you all over."

"I'm here. What's up? Do you need help with something?"

Since we've moved here, I've availed myself to Lynn for anything she needs. I want to be a good and helpful daughter.

Her face brightens at my question. "Yes. Do you mind?"

I'm uncertain what she's asking me to do until I lower my gaze downward. In her hands, she's holding a necklace.

"Oh, sure." I approach her and take the necklace out of her hands. "Wow, I love it. Is this opal?"

"It is."

"Where did you get the necklace? I love it." I've always been into jewelry, but never able to afford pieces I love.

Evan keeps asking me if there's any jewelry I'd want on special occasions, such as my birthday, but I keep telling him not to bother, though it's quite tempting. I'd die for an opal necklace like the one Lynn is holding.

She diverts her eyes from me and turns around, expecting me to secure it on her neck. As I hug the necklace around her, she tells me the story of how, years ago, she made a lot of money on tips at the restaurant, then went out to buy herself something special. It was the reward for her hard work.

"Did Dad ever buy you jewelry?" I'm curious about what type of husband Jimmy was to her.

"Oh ... no." Pause. "No, Jimmy wouldn't buy me gifts."

"I'm sorry, Mom."

She turns around, and the opal on her neck brings her eyes into more focus. She grabs my shoulders and smiles. "That's okay, sweetheart. I've never had those expectations." I'm hoping she would lean in and give me a kiss, but she doesn't. She lets go of me and walks away.

The front bell rings and I run to open the door. The party should be starting, and people will begin arriving soon. Our serving crew is standing on the doorstep, looking around, admiring our property. The younglings, dressed in a uniform, are open-mouthed and saucer-eyed, and clearly not accustomed to visiting houses this big.

I let them in, and they each find their respective space. The DJ finds the music stand, and the other two tend to food and drink.

Shortly after, the doorbell rings again and now I'm

expecting a slew of guests to arrive. Fred said he was going to arrive a little late because his flight from North Carolina was delayed by several hours. A couple of years after Mary had died, Fred met a woman at a conference and fell in love—something he did not feel for his previous wife. But the problem was that she lived in North Carolina, ways from New Hampshire where we lived, so he ultimately had to choose between her or me.

Of course, she chose her. I expected nothing different. He loved me, but a single man needs a stronger bond outside of his love for a child. I encouraged him to go and pursue the woman and move to North Carolina if need be. Several months later, he was on his way to the state to find suitable housing for both. "If you ever need anything, Lucy, I'm just one flight away. Remember," Fred would say.

At first, it was tough to separate and be all alone in the state, but it also meant I could expand my wings and explore life on my own. So far, so good.

At the door, a few unfamiliar faces are standing, their mouth agape, as if they've seen a ghost. Upon entering the house, they survey the surroundings with astonishment, marveling at the luxuries. They barely notice me standing there while their eyes capture Lynn's new home.

I make a noise to grab their attention, and they break free from their spell, finally realizing my presence. One of them says, "You must be Lucy?"

Out of nowhere, Lynn shows up to greet the guests. "Come on in."

She spread her arms open for a wide hug. One by one, they enter her arms and mumble something into her ear. They all turn to me, and Lynn, with enthusiasm in her voice, introduces me to them. One of them is her old neighbor, Rose, and the other one is her high school friend, Greta with her husband in tow. Lynn hugs them for a long time before they reach out to me and hug me with the same level of energy.

Rose grabs my arm and looks into my eyes. "Oh, my goodness. You are so pretty." Then she squints her eyes and says, "You look just like your father."

CHAPTER 14

LYNN

IT'S BEEN SO LONG since I've been at a party. As far as I can remember, I've never organized a party myself, much less in a mini mansion like this one. I'm grateful that Lucy is here and can help with sorting out all the details.

Before the housewarming party begins, I busily arrange fresh flowers in vases, their vibrant colors adding a touch of warmth to our new home. The scent of food wafts from the kitchen, filling the air with a comforting aroma. I glance at the clock, ensuring everything is in place before our guests arrive. Taking a moment, I step back to admire the inviting atmosphere, eager to welcome friends and family to share in this joyous celebration in our spacious house by the ocean.

People are slowly arriving. Greta, with her new husband, Gerry, and Rose all seemed eager to see the house, and meet Lucy, of course. Rose looks radiant in her summer dress and can barely contain her excitement as she fidgets on the spot, her eyes darting in all directions.

Greta and Gerry go to the kitchen and help themselves with a beer. Lucy is right behind them, asking them questions about who they are and how they know me. She's good at small talk. And she doesn't seem nervous at all. Not like I am.

Eventually, a barrage of questions will begin. People must be curious about my life now that I've turned it upside down and reunited with my daughter. This shit doesn't happen every day. It's a scene straight out of a movie, not something you'd expect from someone you've known for years. I don't blame them.

The first question comes from Rose. "Can you give me a house tour?"

With a firm grip on my arm and intense eye contact, she appears to have something more to say, yet remains silent. She just stares at me and waits for me to invite her.

"Sure, follow me."

We first head upstairs to show her the four bedrooms, each one with an adjacent bathroom. Rose stomps behind me, breathing heavily. She looks stunned by the sight. "My goodness, Lynn. Your house is so beautiful. And so big! Have you gotten used to it yet?"

"Of course. It's so easy to get used to ..." I think of Rose's house and put myself in check, carefully choosing my next words. "... new things." It's better to say that than "a major upgrade." I don't want to offend Rose if it's going to imply her place is a shithole. Which it is.

"I'm so happy for you, Lynn. You deserve the best."

As we descend the stairs, I take her to the sunroom,

and then the kitchen, and then we exit through the French door to see the pool and the view of the ocean. By the pool, Greta, Gerry, and Lucy are talking and laughing, and I feel relieved she is easing into my life. I can tell Greta absolutely loves her, and as they chat, she even grabs Lucy's hand for a moment.

After the brief tour of the house, Rose continues with the questions. "Have you met any of your new neighbors yet?"

I think of the man I met earlier, James, who claimed to have recognized me from Red Urchin. These past few months, all I've wanted is to isolate and escape from my past, but no such luck.

"No, not really."

"That's too bad. With time, I'm sure you will meet everyone on the street." She tilts her head and narrows her eyes. "Oh dear, is everything okay? You look sad."

"Sad? Oh no, I'm not sad. Quite the contrary, I'm happy." I fake a smile.

She takes my hand in hers and comes closer. "I miss you, Lynn. I miss seeing your pretty face around the neighborhood." She smiles. "But maybe you'll let me visit you more often and spend more time with you and Lucy."

I nod. "Of course." I recall how Rose used to visit us and overextend her stay, and part of me feels bad that I've just lied to her. I don't want Rose to visit too often.

She fidgets around, as if looking for something, and turns to me with her narrowed eyes. "Is Jimmy coming?"

A sense of foreboding washes over me at the mention

of Jimmy's name. I've been preparing myself for the questions, but I am still feeling uneasy talking about him. Of all people, of course it's Rose who is going to ask.

Just as I'm about to answer, Lucy materializes out of nowhere. "Rose, can I get you something to drink?"

"Su ... sure, dear," she says, "how about some iced tea?"

"Coming up."

As Lucy turns around and heads for the kitchen, Rose repeats the question, "Where is Jimmy?"

Lucy stops in her tracks and looks over her shoulder, as if waiting for my answer. What does she think she will hear this time? Something different?

Both Rose and I look at Lucy, and I interrupt the awkwardness. "Lucy, honey, can I also have an iced tea? Thank you."

Lucy continues to walk, albeit more slowly. I turn to Rose and feel my cheeks redden. The heat is unbearable outside.

"Jimmy and I are getting divorced." I clear my throat.

Rose's eyes and mouth widen. "What?"

I nod. "They say change in life circumstances can really mess the flow of your marriage." I give a fake smile and nod again.

"Why? What happened?" Rose sounds riddled with concern, as if she's about to cry.

"You know, sudden wealth can be damaging to a couple. Trust can easily be ruined."

"I'm so sorry, Lynn." She grabs my hand and gently

caresses it. "Is that why you were acting so ... nervous when I came to visit you that time?"

The day I killed Jimmy, Rose had knocked on my door to inquire about the loud scream I'd let out as soon as I killed him. I was nervous because I'd just placed Jimmy's body parts in four duffle bags, and she almost discovered them, but, of course, I won't tell her that.

"Yes. Yes, Rose. Things went downhill fast after I won the lottery."

Lucy returns with an iced tea in each hand and passes one to each of us. Just when I think that her arrival will pivot the conversation topic, Rose turns to me and continues with her goddamn questions. "Where is Jimmy these days?"

They both stare at me as I regulate the internal anger rising inside me. The nosy Rose hasn't changed a bit. My cheeks flush with even hotter, and I feel I'm about to faint.

"How should I know?" I shake my head in dismissal. "All I know is that we're getting divorced and just waiting for the court to schedule a hearing. My lawyer says that can take a while."

I'd thought I was ready to face the questions about Jimmy, but now I realize I've undermined myself.

Just before Rose asks another question, Greta and Gerry barge in, bringing some relief.

"Lynn, come on out. You've got more guests outside," Greta says.

When I turn around and head outside, I notice Lucy

standing in one place like a statue and boring her eyes into me. She looks like she has a lot more questions for me.

AS LYNN WALKS BY ME, she brushes her shoulder hard against mine. I wonder if she did it on purpose, just to stick it to me, but then she stops and turns around to apologize.

"Oh, I'm so sorry, dear."

She comes near and grabs my arm. Her eyes are droopy with guilt.

"It's okay, Mom." I roll my eyes at her like it's no big deal.

"I'm going outside to greet guests. Come join."

She gazes at me, then at Rose. She looks like she really wants to peel me away from Rose, which, as she'd realize if she knew anything about reverse psychology, is what makes me do the exact opposite.

"I'll be right there." I look at Rose as I say it. The old woman stands there with her head tilted. We both understand that we must get to know each other better.

"Fine." Lynn turns around and hastens her steps to the

backyard where new guests await. Both Rose and I follow her jerky moves, then Rose breaks the awkward silence.

"Why don't we sit somewhere and chat? I'd love to get to know you better."

It doesn't appear that any of my friends have arrived, and Fred and his wife are late anyway, so I resolve to talk to Rose and to satisfy her curiosity.

She grabs my hand and pulls me toward the guest room. We sit next to each other. Rose is still holding her iced tea and sipping it through the straw. Her slurps are loud and annoying, but I say nothing. I remind myself I have to behave well while in the company of Lynn's friends. She puts the glass down on the coaster on the table and gives a fake smile.

"So, what do you do?" Her eyes are wide with anticipation.

Of all the questions she asks, this is the first one that comes to mind? Why the fuck do people need to know what others do for a living? Is that some kind of measurement of a character or personality? I want to smack this woman senseless, but I give her a smile back, just as fake as hers.

"I work as an executive assistant for a Chief Financial Officer at a major corporation."

"Wooow." Rose's eyes grow even wider. "You must be so smart."

"Ah, thanks." I give her a small smile.

If she only knew the type of jobs I've had. Starting as a

barista at Starbucks, then becoming a cashier at Macy's, and eventually settling into the enjoyable role of a dog walker. And the last one at a real estate office, where I got fired. But an executive assistant is the last thing I'd be qualified for. I've finished high school and some college, but I never had an interest in buckling down and working hard toward finishing school. I was planning on returning to education, but when I lost my mom (my other mom), I lost all my motivation.

Rose doesn't need to know my resume. It's none of her business. Plus, the lady seems a little too nosy.

Suddenly, my phone chimes and I take it out of my pocket to find a text message from Fred.

Hey, sweetheart, it looks like our flight has been canceled because of the big storm in NC. I'm so sorry but looks like we won't make it for the party.

My heart sinks. I tuck my phone in my pocket and tell myself I will still force myself to have a good time despite my dad and his new lady not coming.

The music is blasting through the air, thumping the beats and drowning out people's voices. The music is cheerful, but incongruent with people's faces. I expected heartfelt laughter coming from every corner of the house, but everyone looks so serious.

Rose stares at me still and waits for me to tell her the news.

"Is that Jimmy?" She looks in the direction where I put my phone.

"Jimmy?" I get startled by the mention of his name. Her question strikes me as odd. It seems like she's after something, like she's trying to get information out of me. Or maybe she wants to talk about him. I should take that opportunity. "Oh. Jimmy. No." I shake my head.

She tilts her head left and right. *What a weirdo.* I flutter my eyelashes to bat out the awkward silence, and then something occurs to me. Rose knows both Lynn and Jimmy well. For fuck's sake, they have lived next to each other for decades. She probably knows all their life milestones, something I'd never have access to unless I ask. She can be the gate to all my questions if I just learn how to open it.

I muster all the strength and stare back at Rose.

"What is it, dear?" she says.

"I've never met Jimmy. And I'd love to know more about him if you don't mind sharing with me. What is he like?"

She delights in this question and puts the biggest smile, relaxing her shoulders. "Oh. Yes. Jimmy. He was like a son to me. Wonderful, wonderful guy."

When I met Jimmy at McDonald's for the first time, I wouldn't quite describe him as "wonderful." The impression that Jimmy made on Rose must have been a rare incident. He owed her nothing, so I bet that was easy for him. I nod to show my interest and let her continue.

"Jimmy and Lynn are a very special couple. Or were, I guess. They kept to themselves. They were, you know ... quiet for a happy couple."

"Happy?" I repeat. I'd never suspect they were happy together.

"Yes. Yes." Rose scratches her nose and looks in another direction. "They didn't seem to socialize a lot, but they spent a lot of time together. Walks on the beach, BBQs in the backyard … that kind of thing."

"I see. Did you attend their BBQs?"

"Oh, yes. I'd bring a salad and dessert and we would hang out in their backyard all afternoon." She shakes her head lightly, as if reminiscing those days.

"You must miss seeing Lynn all the time, now that she lives in this house."

Rose nods and makes a sad face. "I do. I really do. We were like a family."

"But you can still hang out together regardless, right?" I bite my lip and then go right for it. "Do you see Jimmy often?"

She looks down at the floor as if she is pondering, then looks at me with her eyebrows knitted together. "You know, not really. Lynn said he'd go to some places often and stay for a while. But he always returned home."

I'm intrigued. Where was Jimmy going and why? As a car mechanic, he couldn't be going to conferences or traveling for work.

"Did you know where he was going?"

She shakes her head and says, "No. He never told me."

And you never asked. What a surprise!

"When was the last time you saw Jimmy?"

She's back to staring at the floor, pondering hard. Her

gaze returns to me, and she finally utters, "You know, now that you ask. It's been a while. Quite a while since I've seen your dad."

LYNN

I PEER inside and see Rose and Lucy chatting away. They're sitting too close to each other, and I see Rose touching Lucy's arm. Ugh. Rose is a snake. She knows the art of charming someone until she discovers all their secrets. Hopefully, Lucy will realize it sooner than later.

Nevertheless, my biggest concern is that they will discuss the issue that enrages me and amplifies my paranoia: Jimmy. Lucy has been so obsessed about Jimmy not replying to her messages, and she's bound to question Rose about him, knowing she'd likely to be a less biased source that I would be. Rose, having a big mouth, will volunteer all the information, no doubt. But Rose doesn't know the full story—thankfully.

I pinch my opal necklace Jimmy bought for me as my last gift before he died and roll it between my fingers until someone grabs me from behind. I jump up, startled.

I turn around and see Barbara standing there with a wide smile brightening her face. She is dressed to the nines, her gray hairs covered in freshly made highlights and her red dress emphasizing her beautiful curves. It's the Barbara I have seen rarely, and she looks stunningly beautiful. Behind her is the whole restaurant crew. They come over one by one and offer a hug. Apparently, they've closed the restaurant for a couple of hours, so they can attend our party.

"Look at you, you look so wonderful." Barbara spreads her arms for a big hug, and I sink right in, appreciating the gesture. It's the familiar feeling of being held by someone I've known someone for years. Good, bad or the ugly, I knew exactly what I was getting with Barbara. And now that I'm not working for her anymore, and matching—or maybe even exceeding her wealth—we're more like peers now. It feels good.

My eyes well up with happy tears. I wipe them at once, surprised my former colleagues' gesture would make me so emotional. Before I can offer food and drinks, everyone scatters around like a coop of chickens, pecking around, exploring my new home.

Barbara is still standing in her spot, looking at me with a sense of pride.

"Look at you, my dear. Your house is beautiful." She reaches for my hand and squeezes it. "I can't wait to see the rest of it. And meet your daughter, of course."

"I can't wait for you to meet her as well."

"She sounded lovely on the phone when she ordered food for catering. She strikes me as smart and ambitious."

People always have a precise term to characterize Lucy

when they first encounter her, but I'm still unsure how to describe her accurately. Getting to know someone to the core is a process, I tell myself. Although my inner voice urges me to be patient in getting to know Lucy, a part of me doubts that goodness is her sole character. But, of course, I won't act against her or express my thoughts and feelings in front of other people. Lucy is my daughter, after all.

"You're going to love Lucy," I reassure her.

"Where is she?"

I scan the space around and no longer see either Lucy or Rose. Did they walk somewhere together? I'm awfully suspicious of those two plotting something mysterious behind my back. I brush the thought to the side while I concentrate on finding my daughter. In the periphery of my eye, I see unfamiliar people arriving, and I gather they must be her friends. Lucy told me earlier that Fred and his partner could no longer make it, and while I pretended to be disappointed, it was the best news I heard all day. I didn't want to subject myself to meeting the man who raised my daughter. I should be grateful, but it hurts too much to even think about it.

Lucy shows up out of nowhere to greet her friends. As soon as they come close, they all scream in unison, jumping up and down, creating a circle and jumping around.

"Holy shit, Luc," one says, "this is where you live?"

Lucy's face shines. "Can you believe it?"

One of her friends looks indifferent. Her face remains

cold as she gazes at the house. She doesn't seem impressed by Lucy's new home.

Barbara and I are cemented to our spots, watching the joyous spectacle. But when I look at Barbara more closely, her face turns white, devoid of all color, while she stares open-mouthed at Lucy.

I turn to her and grab her hand. "Barb, are you okay?"

"Yeah ... yeah."

"Are you sure? You look like you saw a ghost."

She swallows a lump in her throat and excuses herself to the kitchen to find a drink.

Why is Barbara acting so strange? Does she recognize Lucy from somewhere else, maybe some questionable place I shouldn't know about? I want to run after Barbara to sort this out, to find out about her reaction, but seconds later, Lucy and her friends are marching their way toward me, their faces etched in curiosity.

"Mom, meet my friends."

Lucy is standing on the end, beaming. She's gazing at her friends, but they're all expecting me to say something, or to deliver a great line.

I shake myself out of stupor and finally find my voice. "Hello, Lucy's friends. Welcome! I'm Lucy's mom."

CHAPTER 17

LYNN

LUCY'S EYELASHES keep fluttering at a rapid speed. She seems overly nervous or excited. Or both. One of her hands is clenched in the other, and she's squeezing it hard. All the blood has drained from it, leaving a white mark. Lucy turns to her friends and introduces them all, one by one. I pay little attention to their names or looks. I've zoned out, processing what just transpired with Barbara.

Something strange just happened here, and I'd like to know what it is.

I gaze at the kitchen and see Barbara talking to someone whose back is turned to me. I'll have to catch her before she goes back to the restaurant.

"Mom. Mom!" Lucy's voice shakes me out of my thoughts. "Dan is asking you a question."

I turn to all her friends. Their eyes widen at me, like I'm some kind of miracle and they're waiting for me to do something amazing. When I scan their faces, I can't quite spot Dan since I wasn't paying attention to their names during the introductions. To salvage the situation, I wave them to the table nearby and say, "Why don't we sit down and talk, shall we? I'd love to get to know my daughter's friends better."

I turn around and trudge over to the table, feeling steps following me behind. Lucy sits next to me, and all her friends follow suit. We sit in a circle, our eyes darting all over the place, and a young man repeats his question. "How did you win the lottery?"

An involuntary burst of laugher comes out of my mouth. I was expecting questions related to my reunion with Lucy, not this. Lottery? I guess winning big is everyone's dream. Maybe his question shouldn't surprise me at all.

I stick to the highlights. "I walked into the convenience store, asked for a ten-dollar scratch ticket, and the next thing you know, I won five million dollars." I smile and gaze at them.

"Wow," Dan says.

"What convenience store?" another male friend with a freckled face asks, as if planning on trying his luck later.

"There's one across the beach, next to a gas station."

He's quiet at first, as if making a mental note, then he says, "Cool."

I remember the day I walked into that convenience store. It was early May, and the day was gorgeous, just like today. The night before, Jimmy and I got into a nasty fight. I'd expected him to hurt me, like he always did when he was disagreeable, but he minded his business instead for the rest of the night. The restless feeling of contempt for him rose inside me. I was hating every second spent with Jimmy, realizing how he was dragging me and my life down. I had to do something. The lottery was an option, but never in my wildest dreams did I think it would pan out and become a reality.

I don't want to be reminded of those days, but I remember the day I won like it happened yesterday. And I will never forget it. I also remember the fear of being discovered and later beaten, because I was hiding something valuable from Jimmy.

I sigh with relief and look at my beautiful home, then gaze at my daughter on my left, and convince myself everything worked out as it should.

Feeling confident, I turn to all her friends and ask, "So, how do you all know each other?"

"These are my college friends, Mom," Lucy chimes in.

"We took same classes in the sophomore year," one of her female friends adds.

I'm embarrassed that I don't know what Lucy studied in college. Something marketing-related, but I wouldn't bet my life on it. Or ... maybe arts. Who the hell knows? Either way, I don't think I can get deep into this conversation. I'll just embarrassed the hell out of myself.

"It's great you guys are still friends. You all seem like a friendly bunch."

They giggle and gaze at each other, as if reminiscing about the good times from college.

"So, tell me," I continue. "What do you all like about Lucy?"

Instant silence ensues, and only music projecting through the house and yard echoes. Their smiles fade away as they exchange bewildered looks, clearly puzzled by my question.

Was my question odd?

It's possible my question is inappropriate, but hell, so many years of isolation will ruin one's sense of the social etiquette. Now I'm fidgeting in my chair, hoping for a rescue. Lucy, as if she reads my mind, reaches for a glass in front of her and lifts it up in the air.

"I'd like to say a little toast." She smiles, but I wonder if this is just her way of deescalating the awkward situation. She's smooth, if that's her intention. We're all looking at Lucy, waiting for her to deliver a speech. She closes her eyes for a second, then opens them, only to place her gaze somewhere in a far distance.

"Thank you all for gathering here today to witness a moment that has been twenty-five years in the making—a moment of reunion, of rediscovery, and of profound emotion. Today, I stand before you, not just as an individual, but as a daughter who has found her way back to a mother she never knew existed."

Lucy looks at me and gives me a smile filled with pride. We all stay silent, expecting Lucy to continue. I'm curious as to what she has to say.

"As I reflect on this incredible journey, I'm overwhelmed with a mix of emotions that words can hardly express. Twenty-five years ago, the paths of my mother and me diverged in ways neither of us could have foreseen. Life took us on separate journeys, and for most of my existence, I was unaware of the incredible woman who gave me life.

Today, as fate would have it, our paths have converged once again. The universe has conspired to bring us together, and I stand in front of the woman whose blood runs through my veins." She grins at me, and I swallow the sudden lump in my throat.

"To my mother, who didn't know I still lived, I want to express the gratitude and love that has been building within me for a quarter of a century. Life has tested us, but now we stand face to face, ready for a new beginning."

Suddenly, she halts her speech like someone has flipped a switch. She props herself up in the chair and looks in the house's direction. She clearly sees something that catches her eye, and I sense the urgency in her to address it.

"Excuse me for a second." Lucy moves the chair out of her way and hastens in the house's direction. My eyes follow her until her small stature disappears behind the kitchen door.

The awkward silence returns. All her friends are looking at me, expecting me to say something. I feel my cheeks burning and my world spinning around like a roller-coaster. I'd better say something. I clap my hands together, glance at each person, and exclaim, "Let's go get some food, shall we?"

I NEARLY TRIP and fall as I run toward the kitchen. Is that Evan I see in the house? Am I fucking dreaming right now? No, it can't be. I haven't told him where I live. I'd kill him if he stopped over.

I walk into the kitchen to find the intruder, but the space is hopping around and I'm feeling disoriented. The kitchen is always the most popular spot at parties. I'm certain Evan was roaming around, looking for something, exploring the space. But he's nowhere to be found.

I walk to the family room and take a peek at the sunroom, but they're both empty. I breeze past the couple of bedrooms on the first floor and don't see or sense any commotion. The kitchen is where things are happening. Greta and Rose are enthralled in their conversation while Greta's husband stands next to them, holding a plate of food. All Lynn's former restaurant coworkers are standing on the other side of the kitchen, chatting away and laughing.

But Evan isn't here.

Now I'm certain it wasn't him after all. My recurring fear of Evan suddenly materializing is playing tricks on my mind.

I stand in the middle of the kitchen and let out a breath that brings me calm. The caterer approaches me holding a tray of food and offers me scallops wrapped in bacon. I shake my head and thank him. I've never much cared for either seafood or bacon. It's the worst possible combination.

Now that I realize Evan hasn't shown up and all of this is my imagination, I reflect on my last interactions with Lynn and my friends. What was up with Lynn? Had she never been to a party before? God, she's embarrassing. She's clearly incapable of having a meaningful conversation and seems way too anxious to connect with others. If she wants to make or keep her friends, she needs to step up her game.

Someone taps my left shoulder, and I turn around and see an unfamiliar face staring at me.

"Hi," she says.

"Hi?"

"My name is Barbara. You and I spoke on the phone the other day when you ordered food."

"Ah, yes." Relief sooths my frazzled nerves. This woman appears to be normal and pleasant. Mom needs to stick with people like her. "Nice to meet you."

"Lovely to meet you as well, dear." She lands me a hug,

as if she's been waiting for this moment for a long time. "I can't wait to get to know you better."

"Me too," I say, enthusiasm evident in my voice.

"I've known Lynn for almost thirty years. Wonderful woman. You're so lucky to have a mother like her."

Thirty years is a long time to get to know someone. Wonderful woman? I guess I'll take her word for it.

"Yeah, you know, we're still getting to know each other. It's been only a few months since we reunited."

"Of course, of course," she says. "Even if you know someone all your life, you still get to learn about them. You should enjoy the ride."

"I'm trying." I give her a small smile, not quite sounding confident in my assertion.

She narrows her eyes and says, "I think I've seen you before."

A spark of curiosity lights up within me. I tilt my head, squinting a bit, trying to place where our paths might have crossed. It feels like a gentle puzzle, and I can't help but smile, intrigued by the possibility of a shared connection. I respond with a friendly nod, eager to uncover the mystery behind Barbara's familiar recognition.

Then I remember.

I swallow a lump in my throat. Those were the days when I would follow Lynn around like a shadow. I found myself at Red Urchin simply because she would go there, and I'd follow her lead. I wonder if Barbara remembers me from there. But seriously? This woman must have a razor-sharp memory given how many customers and people she sees on a daily. Why exactly would she remember me? Besides, I couldn't have been there for longer than ten minutes.

But I confess anyway and tell her I used to follow Lynn and had found myself at Red Urchin one time.

She shakes her head and says, "No. No. That's not it. I'm sure I've seen you somewhere else. Someone told me about you. I'm pretty sure."

She gazes to the side as if thinking hard, then looks at me. Her eyes are wide, and her face has drained of all the red she had just moments ago. She opens her mouth wide, then says. "Oh, my God. That's you. Isn't it?"

I don't understand what she's implying. I'm growing wary that something sinister is at stake, and I'm not liking it at all.

Just as I'm about to interrogate her about what she exactly means, Lynn appears out of nowhere, placing her hand on both of our shoulders.

"Looks like you two finally met!" Lynn's cheer is undeniable. "How about we go outside? I want to say a few words to our guests."

THE ATMOSPHERE in the house is stifling. Despite the festive appearance, the guests exude a somber aura, as if they've gathered for a funeral rather than a reunion celebration. I feel a pressing need to break free from this oppressive mood. I wish I could change the atmosphere, but the heavy mood is like a black cloud that won't lift.

Hurrying through the kitchen, I escape to the backyard. The afternoon heat is relentless, and beads of sweat form on my forehead.

Standing in the center of the patio, I beckon everyone closer. "Come in, please. Come closer."

The crowd converges, some holding drinks and sipping as they approach. Among them are unfamiliar faces—likely Lucy's friends. Now encircled by party attendees, I notice more unfamiliar faces than familiar ones. Rose stands at the back, offering a smile and nodding, though her attempts at encouragement fall short.

Taking command of the situation becomes imperative. I can't let my rattled nerves disrupt the proceedings. Lucy stands beside me, her narrowed eyes reflecting confusion. She clutches her iced tea glass, twisting it in her hands as if trying to wring it dry. Clearing my throat, I survey the circle and begin speaking. All eyes are on me.

"Um, hi. Thank you all for being here. I must admit, this is strange for me. I just discovered that the amazing person standing in front of me is my daughter. My daughter. I still can't quite wrap my head around it."

I shake my head, privately rolling my eyes at the involuntary gesture stemming from nervousness. Clearing my throat again, I press on.

"I guess life has this funny way of throwing curveballs at you, and finding out I have a daughter after twenty-five years is definitely one of those. I mean, who would have thought, right? Not me, that's for sure."

A nervous chuckle escapes me, prompting uncertain glances among the crowd. I resolve to push through, aiming to express heartfelt gratitude for this unexpected reunion.

"So, to my daughter—wow, that feels weird and wonderful to say—I want to say, um, hi. I didn't know you existed, and that's, well, a lot to take in. But here we are, and you seem like an incredible person. I hope I didn't mess things up too much by not knowing you were out there." I allow myself a breath before diving back in.

"I suppose I should apologize for not being around all those years. It's not like I was intentionally avoiding you; I just didn't know. And now, well, we have a lot of catching up to do, right? It's like we're starting a relationship, but, you know, with a twenty-five-year gap."

A chuckle from the crowd emerges. I close my eyes, feeling the impending descent into embarrassment, but I rally myself. As I open my eyes, the bright sun offers renewed hope that my next words won't cause irreparable damage.

"To be honest, I'm not sure what I'm doing here or what I'm supposed to say. But I want you to know that, awkward as it may be, I'm really glad we found each other. I mean, how many people get a second chance at something like this, right? I hope we can figure this out together. I may not have been there for the first twenty-five years, but I'm here now, and, uh, I want to be a part of your life. So, here's to, um, new beginnings and, uh, figuring out how to be a family. Thanks for being patient with me, and, um, let's see where this takes us."

I look around to see all the faces intently looking at me.

"Yeah, that's it. Thanks."

Before shame takes hold, Lucy steps in front of me, offering a giant hug. Seconds later, the sound of applause fills the space, and someone whistles loudly. Lucy's embrace feels like a welcome reprieve from everything I'm feeling.

"Oh, Mom, what a brilliant speech. I love that we've found each other."

In the corner of my eye, I spot Barbara standing still, the redness of her dress an undeniable distraction.

Zooming in on her face, I shiver when I notice her mouthing something to me. Narrowing my eyes for better focus, as Barbara mouths again, her silent words send me into shock.

If my eyes are correct, I believe she said, "It's all a lie."

LYNN

I RUN to my bedroom to compose myself after that little speech and the words Barbara whispered in my direction. Everything seems so overwhelming. I wish I could tell all our guests to go home, but that would make everything so much worse. I spread out on my bed and practice slow breathing. Good chi in, bad chi out. All those people staring at me flash in front of my eyes, and I blink a few times to abet those images.

Feeling lost, I walk to the window for a change of scenery. My bedroom faces our front yard, so I can't see any of our guests in the back or what is happening at the party. No one comes after me. I imagine Lucy laughing and chattering with her friends, overridden by joy and happiness.

The sight of a man standing near our gate interrupts my thoughts. He seems to be gazing through our gate, trying to catch a glimpse of what's happening at the house. I can't tell from here whether I recognize him or not.

I lean up on my toes, stretching myself by a couple of inches, but I still can't see clearly enough. The man just stands there, not moving, looking through the gate.

My heart races. Who is he, and what does he want?

I cup my hands around my face and squint to see better when the man makes a couple of steps to his left, exposing his entire face. The sight of James, the cop, makes me flinch.

Fear turns into anger, propelling me to go outside and face him. I need to know what he wants from me. I swiftly move through the house with hardly anyone noticing me. The front door is wide open for incoming guests, though I doubt anyone else is coming, unless unannounced. I walk through the door and slam it, sending vibrations through the house.

I nearly fall as my steps rush across the ground. Facing James makes me nervous, but it is a necessity. I need to know what he wants from me. He's standing on the other side of the gate, his fingers entangled between the bars. He sports a curious smile on his face, and his eyebrows raise when I come closer.

I stop right in front of him, just a few short inches from the gate. "What is it you want? Are you stalking me?"

Only when I hear my voice do I realize the extent of my rage. I've had enough of being tormented by one James; more of it by another one is unacceptable.

"I see you're having a little party." The smirk on his face isn't going away.

"And?"

"I was just in the neighborhood and wanted to drop by."

He definitely does not live on this street. So, what the hell is he doing "dropping by"?

"Why? Why are you doing this?"

His head snaps in surprise, and he moves away from the bars. "What am I doing?"

"You're stalking me. That's what."

His face morphs to serious and his wrinkles become more pronounced as he bores his gaze to me. "You remember me, don't you? But you're pretending like you don't. It bothers me and I don't know what game you're playing."

He gapes at me as I stare back at him. "I don't know what you're talking about."

"Yes, you do. You're the one who has served me the chicken parmesan for the millionth time at Red Urchin. And you even know me by name. Why would you pretend you didn't know me?"

Gosh, he sounds like a psycho. A dangerous mix of hurt and menace projects from his eyes. I shake my head in disbelief.

"I know you're married to Jimmy." I feel like a knife slices me in half at the mention of Jimmy's name. "I haven't seen him around. Does he know you're a fucking liar?"

Maybe he's been looking for Jimmy all this time. But I don't care.

"Now, that's enough!" I say through my clenched teeth.

As I'm about to tell him to leave and never come back, a voice from behind me comes into focus. It's Lucy. I hadn't heard her steps moving in our direction.

"Everything okay here?" She looks at the intruder and nods. "I'm Lucy. Hi."

He nods and says nothing.

"James was just about to leave. He wanted to stop by and say hello." My eyes are still transfixed on the man, serving more than a threat.

"Oh, would you like to come to the party? There's plenty of food." Lucy sounds happy in her naivete.

It's all my fault that she's clueless. Though, I wish I could live without fear or preconceived notions like Lucy does. I wish I could erase my history, starting at twenty until now. I'd be a lot happier and less worried about the world I live in.

I turn to Lucy, widening my eyes in disbelief that she'd invite someone who was a stranger to her. "Like I said, James was on his way. Maybe next time. Right, James?"

"Right."

We both put a fake smile on, then James turns around and disappears from the hedges nestled between the gate and our neighbor's property.

"Let's go, Mom." Lucy takes my hand and leads me back to the house.

I turn around to ensure there are no traces of James and hope to never set my eyes on him ever again.

AT FIVE O'CLOCK in the evening, the guests go home. The sudden quiet is a stark difference from the loud music and people roaming around. We've returned the house to its previous clean state. It looks like the party had never even taken place.

Before everyone left, I invited my friends to stay over for a swim in the pool, but they looked uncomfortable and came up with a random excuse not to stay. When they first arrived, they were all impressed by the house, except for Rebecca. Rebecca is the exception in my college friend group, being both from a wealthy family and unimpressed by the house. She'd surveyed the house with indifference, fitting right in, nothing appearing as unusual to her.

They'd all driven a long way to be at our house-warming party. Having them here feels like a precious gift, and I'm thankful for the effort they made to be present. But none of them accepted my offer to stay over for the night. They'd all rather go home and drive for hours.

I pulled Rebecca aside to ask her why she was in such a rush. Of all people, I'd expect her to stay longer. During college years, she was my bestie, and we shared the same dorm room. She became one of those friends I could confess my darkest and deepest secrets to, and she'd keep them to herself.

I looked up at Rebecca as a voice of reason, the only person to tell me things like they are. Brutal honesty and all. And sometimes, the truth as she spoke it stung, but deep down, I knew she was right.

Like the time I called to tell her about Evan. I'd been smitten by him, and he took an immediate liking to me, which was unusual. I told Rebecca how Evan and I created an immediate connection, and she'd screeched in happiness over the phone until I revealed the next fact.

"The only trouble is that he's not our age."

"What do you mean? How old?"

"If I were to guess, he's in his forties." I cleared my throat. "Late forties."

There was a pause on the other side of the line, then a sigh.

"Luc. Sorry to break the news. I don't want to burst your bubble, but the guy is two generations apart. It will never work out."

"Really?" I squinted, hoping to hear something different, but Rebecca reaffirmed her position by continuing her lecture.

"Yes. I've known other couples with a big age differ

ence, and they look so out of place. Miserable. I don't want your life to turn that way."

I felt the weight of her words, only because they rang true. If there was any hope of having a meaningful relationship with Evan, it is now diminished by Rebecca's advice to stay away from him. We don't talk about Evan anymore, as I don't want Rebecca's opinions to cloud my feelings. After all, it's just that—her opinions.

But now, I wonder how she feels after meeting Lynn. She'd glanced at her with a strange, menacing look, exchanging eye rolls with our other friends. When I asked why she wouldn't stay, she'd creased her eyebrows and looked at me funny. "Lucy, sorry, but your mom is like super weird."

"What? Weird?"

"Don't take it the wrong way, but there's something about her that doesn't sit well with me. I don't know what it is." She shrugged her shoulders.

In that instance, my cheeks flushed, as anger rose inside me. "What are you saying, Becca? She's my mom, for fuck's sake. I know she's not perfect but come on. Give her a chance!"

Rebecca shrugged her shoulders again, turned around, and hastened her steps to follow my other friends moving toward the front gate.

I wanted to stop her and probe further, but against my better judgment, I let it go. If I'm being honest with myself, the party has been a disappointment. Not only did some people not show up at all, like they said they would, but the general atmosphere was heavy. Not to mention that Lynn acted all weird, and I don't know what that's all about.

I can only have so much empathy. Sure, the discovery that her daughter was still alive must be shocking. But now, it's time to embrace the reality and share some mutual love. Lynn has odd ways of showing love sometimes.

After the party, I find Lynn sitting at the kitchen table, her head down. When I get closer, I see her gazing down at the phone in her hands.

"Hey, Mom."

She gets startled and jumps out of her chair. "I didn't hear you coming."

"What are you doing?" I ask.

"Just catching up with my email." She looks at me tentatively, then drops her head down back to the phone.

"Okay." I stand next to the table, trying to connect. "What did you think of the party?"

She glances at me, then moves her gaze back to the phone. "It was ... lovely. Really wonderful to meet some of your friends."

"They were happy to meet you, as well."

That's definitely not true, but I can't let my friends' judgment of my mother cloud my own feelings for her. Yes, we are still getting to know each other, but I still feel an inherent love for her, the kind I used to have for my adopted mother. It's the feeling I can't explain easily. It happens naturally, similar to the break of dawn. There is no other choice.

"So, Mom. What is with your friend Barbara? She seems nice, but ... I don't know. She was acting a little strange."

Lynn's head snaps toward me and she looks at me, her eyes etched in fear. "Why do you say that? Did she say anything to you?"

I shake my head. "Well, she claims she has met me before. I don't know where she'd get that from." I let out a nervous laugh.

Lynn's eyes narrow at me, then they move left and right at a rapid speed, as if she's computing the information.

"Know you?" she says. "How would she know you? Where from?"

Lynn's right hand shakes, and she covers it with her left to stop it from shaking. Something has triggered her. I shrug my shoulders. "Beats me."

I could tell her I'd once stalked her at Red Urchin, but Barbara doesn't seem to think she knows me from there. Plus, I don't want to bring up the subject of stalking Lynn again. That was messed up, I admit, and if I could do it all over again, I'd think twice about how to approach Lynn.

But what's done is done. I can't change the past.

"Barbara is a fine woman, but I'd steer clear of her," Lynn says.

"Oh. But why? Do you have something against her?"

Lynn's eyes roll over like she's about to have a seizure, but she composes herself quickly and looks at me. "I wouldn't bring this up normally, but she's the one who introduced me to drugs." Lynn looks at me with defeat on her face, then goes back to checking her email, or whatever else she's doing.

"I didn't know." I pause and think about this new information. "So, if you have a grudge against her, how is it you're still friends?"

The tension is palpable as a mutual stare commences. Lynn seems to be caught and unprepared for the question. Her go-to gesture when she's nervous always seems to be shaking her head and rolling her eyes.

"Well, it wasn't always bad with her," Lynn says. "She gave me my job when I was desperate."

"When was that?" I don't wait.

"I can't remember." She shakes her head. "Maybe thirty years ago?"

"Thirty...?" I catch and stop myself in time to not sound like a judgmental asshole. Lynn had the same job for thirty years? I sure as shit hope I don't follow in her footsteps.

This is all too much to take. Getting to know Lynn better is tough, especially when I don't like what I hear. While we're on the subject of employment, I redirect our conversation and make an announcement.

"Listen, Mom." I pause. "I have a new job. I start this Monday."

"Oh, dear." She lifts her head for a second. "That's such great news. I'm so happy for you."

But as her eyes stare back at me, I see emptiness in them. I wonder how happy she really is.

"Okay, well. I'm going out to do some errands and get ready for it. Are you going to be okay at home alone?"

"Yeah, totally. I don't even know why you'd ask."

I ask because I care about her. I don't know what's going on with her, but I hope to get to the bottom of it soon.

I say bye to Lynn before getting ready for my brief trip. As I apply makeup in the bathroom, something occurs to me. Lynn never asked about my new job or how I came to find it, or even what it is.

But part of me is relieved, because it's all a lie, anyway. I just want to escape from the house occasionally. She will never know or suspect. Besides, I want to show her I'm not here to leech on her wealth.

Lynn ought to have a good and admirable daughter.

I PEER behind the curtain of my bedroom window and spot Lucy's car slowly moving down the driveway then through the gate before turning to the left, leaving a heavy cloud of smoke behind. It looks like she hasn't changed the oil in her car for ages, and Jimmy would hate her for that. As a meticulous auto mechanic, he'd always complained about how people didn't care for their cars as well as they should. But I won't complain or say anything about it. She might take it personally. I'm sure she'd be receptive to my advice, like she was about putting the sunscreen on, but if I'm too preachy all the time, she'll hate me for it.

We're not there yet.

I wait ten minutes for Lucy to get far enough, so I don't have the chance of running into her. I grab the car keys from the kitchen island and zoom through the hallway to get to my car in the garage. I'm still reeling from the image of Barbara whispering in my direction, telling me it's all lies. I didn't have time to probe her while at the party, but I don't want to wait another minute to confront her.

Slowly, I drive through the streets of Hampton, lowering the side window to enjoy the ocean breeze. It's an early evening, and late in the summer, that the main beach isn't bustling as it usually is in the dead of the summer. When kids go back to school, things become somewhat desolate around here.

I'm grateful for that, because I don't want to fight traffic on my way to Red Urchin. My body is charged with the anticipation of what Barbara has to say about her despicable words. I have the right to know what she meant. Just reflecting on it sends shivers down my spine.

I pull into the parking lot behind Urchin, and memories flood through me instantly.

When I first got the waitressing job here thirty years ago, the place didn't look like this at all. The outside restaurant walls had a darker color, and the parking lot was a covered in pebbles and dirt. Barbara's parents, still alive then, invested a lot in the property by changing the wall color to a more cheerful orange and paving the parking lot, allowing tens of parking slots for their visitors.

Those early days were a lot more memorable than those that preceded. Once Barbara introduced me to Skull, things went downhill. There were multiple instances where my life was hanging by a thread. Yet thanks to Skull, the same person who helped me get there, I survived.

I wipe the palms of my hands against my dress, pull the visor down, and look at myself in the mirror. Make-up makes me look younger. The absence of it makes me look like an old, worn-out woman nobody wants to associate with. Maybe I need to use it more often from now on?

I exit the car and head through the restaurant door. The level of activity indoors is just right, not too much to handle. I know it too well as a former waitress. Barbara has hired new staff, and I don't recognize a couple. One of them is the hostess, standing at the podium by the door, holding a menu in her hand. "Welcome to Red Urchin. How many?"

It's the script Barbara has taught every single host to follow.

"I'm not here to have dinner. I need to speak with Barbara."

She turns around, looking for her boss, her eyes darting all over the restaurant. She gives me a puzzled look. "I don't know where she is."

Barbara has a small office in the back of the kitchen, and she'd spend hours there when the restaurant seems less busy.

"I know where to find her."

I breeze by the kitchen and the bathroom, finding myself in front of Barbara's office door. God knows how many times I'd gone knocking on that door, either to air grievances or seek help from her. Most of the time, she was a good listener, and I hope she'll grant me the same hospitality today.

The knuckles of my hand gently reach the door before knocking twice.

"Who is it?" Barbara's voice is undeniable. Stern and annoyed.

"It's Lynn."

Instead of telling me to come in, there's silence. Seconds later, the door opens, and Barbara's head peeks in the gap. "What is it?"

"Can I talk to you for a second?"

She opens the door fully and allows me to come in. She looks surprised to see me, and I don't blame her, since she was at our housewarming just a few hours ago. Since the party, she's swapped her red dress for khaki pants and a T-shirt adorned with the Red Urchin logo in the center. She doesn't look like the same, charming woman who attended our party just a few short hours ago. Lynn is stern and business-like.

I walk through the door hesitantly, feeling as if I'm being summoned by my boss so they can let me know I didn't smile enough in front of our customers today, and wasn't fast enough to approach the table when a customer waved me in. Even though those days are over, the feelings linger, and those images flash in front of my eyes.

Barbara sits back in her chair and gestures to the seat across from hers. "Sit. Tell me. What is there to talk about?" She sounds dismissive.

"I have something specific to ask."

She raises her brows. "You do? I didn't know you and I still have things to discuss." She laughs. She crosses her left leg over the other and crosses her arms on her bosom. "What is it, Lynn? Spit it out."

I take a breath. "It's about the thing you said at the party."

She scrunches up her face, contorting it into one big wrinkle. I don't miss that expression. I've seen it too many times, afraid she'd explode any second in my presence. I clutch onto my purse and muster the courage to say, "I saw you whisper to me, and if I'm not mistaken, you said it was all a lie. What did you mean by it?"

She scoffs and waves her hand at me. "You must be crazy. I didn't say shit to you, much less those words. Sounds like you're imagining things."

I shake my head. "I'm pretty sure you said it, Barb. Can you tell me what you meant? Did you meet Lucy before, prior to the party?"

Barbara spins in her chair, putting her back to me. She leans over her desk, rearranging the items on the desktop. Turning around again to face me, she says, "I can't deny that I might have seen her somewhere, but I have no idea where. It could be the fact that she looks like you when you were younger. A spitting image. Maybe that's it."

My eyes dart all over Barb's face, ensuring she's telling me the truth. She doesn't flinch. Then she takes her gaze off me. "Lynn, hate to say it, but ever since you've won the lottery, you're not the same person. You're a little too high-strung and you worry too much. Why can't you just relax?"

I stay silent.

"I mean, you've got your daughter back," she continues. "Shouldn't you be happy?"

I shrug. "I am happy. But I need reassurance that I can trust you."

"I don't have time for this." Barbara turns around and pretends to be busy on her computer. She looks at me over her shoulder and says, "Please leave. I've got shit to do."

Depleted, I walk through the door and back to my car, contemplating Barbara's words. Why did she regard me with such hostility? Did I strike a chord with her? Could it all be in my head? Maybe Jimmy was right all long.

Maybe I'm just paranoid.

I ARRIVE at Evan's a little after six. I just wanted to get away from the house and smoke pot alone, but when I get there, his car's out the front. He rarely takes time off work. He has one of those jobs that warrants constant communication, check-ins, talking to his guys. In all honesty, I'm not sure what his job is. I don't ask too many questions for the fear of getting too close.

I don't want to get close to anyone because they'd expect something from me. When you take, you also have to give for the relationship equilibrium, but if I am being honest, I'm not much of a giver. At least not in a deep sense. Depths elude me, and I am scared I will reach the bottom.

And when you reach the bottom, it's a hard way to crawl back up.

I enter the house and sing out "hello," but I get no response. Maybe Evan isn't at home after all. Just as I'm about to enter the kitchen, Evan shows up, looking somewhat disheveled, and looks at me with his sleepy eyes. "Hey. What are you doing here?"

He's topless and looking like a hot mess. I rarely find Evan in this state. I hope he's okay.

"Hey." I give him a smile, as I'm genuinely happy to see him. "I came by to hang out. Is it not a good time?"

He trots over to me and gives me a hug. "Oh, you know you're always welcome here. Any time."

That's what I was afraid he'd say. He might think this is the time I'll change my mind about us. That we'll get closer and maybe have a legitimate relationship. All these months we've been seeing each other, I haven't given an ounce of hope or a sign it would ever happen between us.

But today, his affection feels good. For the very first time, I appreciate that Evan welcomes me and wants my company. I'm feeling overwhelmed and I really need to unwind and hang out with my best friend.

"Thanks, Evan. I've had a bit of a shitty day," I proclaim. I don't tell him we had a party today or that I've met some of Lynn's friends. He'd be hurt about not being invited. Evan takes my hand and pulls me toward his bedroom.

"Come here, sweet thing."

We walk in and plop onto the bed. A bong is sitting on the table. Evan fiddles about with his supply and lights it before taking a deep inhale and passing it onto me. When I do the same, calmness rushes to my head and my body relaxes. Evan extends his arm and brings me closer to him. With my head on his shoulder, I can sense him breathe and feel the pulse of his heart. Today, it's beating faster than usual.

It's as if something has bothered him lately. But Evan is the type of guy who wouldn't divulge his problems. He'd rather listen and be present, showing all the love he can give me. If he could protect me from the entire world, he would. Today, I take advantage of it for the first time, even if a little unwillingly.

"So, Evan, my new mom. She's something else. Let me tell ya," I quip.

I stare at the ceiling, observing its whiteness, emptiness, while Evan caresses my hair with the arm that hugs me. His touch brings me to a different level of calm. It feels like nothing else exists. So, I continue.

"I can't place my finger on it, but she's been acting really strange." I take a puff in and exhale. My eyes rest on a mark on the ceiling as I reflect on my past few weeks of living with Lynn. "I mean, she's nice. She really wants to make me happy and all, but she's just so ... awkward." I laugh.

"I can't come up with a better description," I carry on. "I'm her daughter, and she has all this guilt about not having me for over two decades because drugs fucked her up back then. I just don't know how she's going to move past it." I shake my head even though it's clear Evan isn't facing or watching me.

"I've met her friend Barbara, too."

Evan stops caressing my hair for a second, then continues running his fat fingers through it again. He's probably wondering when I met Lynn's friend, but I've resolved not to tell him about the party. No reason to inflict more wounds on my buddy. "And she ... she's nice, don't get me wrong. But she said she knew me from somewhere, and I have no idea what she's talking about. I mean ..."

And now is the time to go deeper, spill all my beans to Evan. I know he won't judge.

"I mean, I used to follow Lynn everywhere, and once to Red Urchin, where they both worked, but her friend is positive she didn't see me there. So, if she didn't see me there, where the fuck did she see me?"

I turn to Evan, and he's looking straight ahead, his fingers never leaving my hair. His pensive look is making me think he is a good listener, and a sliver of guilt pricks at me that I've treated him the way I have: like a plaything to spend time with.

"Even worse ... even worse," I continue. "I haven't told you that Lynn and my biological dad, Jimmy, are getting divorced. But here's a kick. And it hurts." I know Evan will be the most understanding one of what I'm about to say. "I've been calling and texting Jimmy forever now, and he hasn't returned my calls. What kind of douche ignores their daughter, for fuck's sake?"

At this, I expect Evan to chime in and tell me something from this familiar perspective, but Evan caresses my hair and gives me a quick gaze into my eyes before he diverts it. He looks bruised and worn out. Have I said too much?

Although I'm hesitant to burden him with my grievances, I already feel a sense of relief after opening up to him. It only brings to mind the type of parent he had been and how he suffers from the permanent absence of his son.

We lie like that for a minute or two in silence, but Evan still says nothing in return.

Nothing at all.

On my way home that evening, I drop by the beach to take a quick walk and clear my head. The not-so-distant memories of meeting Lynn come to mind—that moment when we stood face to face for the very first time—and goosebumps form on my arms as I think about how it all played out. It feels surreal. But my expectations were different. I thought we'd wrap each other in love, but it feels nothing like it. Lynn has been stone-cold, nothing like what my adopted mom used to be. Mary was the kind of person who had my photo in her wallet; she was the person who laughed at my jokes and cried at my tears. As I think of her, involuntary tears well up my eyes.

I lie down on the sand and watch the single heavy cloud hover above me. The fog lifts, and the chilly air moves into the coastline. Hints of fall hover in the air, and the idyllic little town is now void of tourists. As my eyes dart across the sky, in a distance, I see a big patch of blue sky swallowed up by the grayness. It feels good to be alive and witness the natural beauty of our planet.

As I watch the waves crush the rocks, a sudden fear comes over me: I don't want to go home, even though it's a place of beauty. I take a look at my phone, curious if Jimmy has tried to call or text me back, but there's nothing. Then a thought crosses my mind that perhaps Lynn might have sent me a cute random text with heart emojis like Mary used to. But there's nothing.

Just a growing sense of dread as I come to terms with who my biological parents are.

IT'S SUNDAY, the day after our housewarming party. Just an ordinary day under the sun.

Lucy and I are sitting in a shady spot by the pool, and there's not much conversation going on between us. She made us lunch earlier—a healthy salad with avocado and hard-boiled eggs and salmon on the side. It was delicious. When I asked her where she learned to cook so well, she said her mom was a skilled cook, and she picked up from her. She said it with pride in her voice and didn't bother to add "adopted" next to the word mother.

Jealousy isn't something I should afford to have in my life. Not related to Lucy. After all, I let her down as a real mother and didn't even know she was alive until just recently. For crying out loud, I signed the paperwork to give her away at birth. I was so drugged, so lost in my world, I didn't know what I was doing. Jimmy didn't help, either. The fact he wanted a son, and not a daughter, sealed Lucy's ultimate fate.

Lucy stands up from her chair and stretches while staring at the ocean. She's so skinny and tiny; she really reminds of me when I was her age. Same build, same hair color, same movements.

"Are you going somewhere?" I ask.

"Yeah, just need to use the toilet."

"Oh, okay. Are you coming back?"

While looking somewhere else, she says, "Yeah, I'll be back."

She ascends the stairs and goes through the kitchen door. I close my eyes for a second and try my best to enjoy this: all of it. The breeze caressing my face; the ocean whooshing by my side; digesting the food my daughter made earlier. An involuntary smile crawls across my face. I'm truly a lucky woman.

But the feeling is fleeting.

A male voice wakes me up from my trance. "Hey there."

When I peel my eyes open, I see a familiar face standing by the pool, staring at me. It's Danny. The cop. The guy who'd found me after the car accident that Jimmy had orchestrated. The cop who came by my house to ask if I was okay and wondered why I fled the hospital like I did after the accident. I couldn't believe it when the cop tried to convince me that rats had eaten my car brakes.

Danny is surveying the house and the yard, his head snapping back in amazement. His uniform looks crisp and neat, and a shiny badge gleams on his chest. He was Jimmy's buddy, I'm sure of it. I think they frequently exchanged favors to avoid getting into trouble. But now that he's here, fear surges up my spine. I control my breathing the best I can, so to hide it.

"Danny?"

"Hey, Lynn." He gives me a small wave.

"How did you get in?" I look toward the side, not that I can see our house's entrance. We keep the front gate locked even during the day, but someone must have left the gate unlocked or open today. Is it Lucy? I must have a serious talk with her about leaving the gate unlocked.

"I just opened the front door and got in." He looks around and adds, "A stunning house you have. I'm jealous. A cop like me could never afford a house like this." He laughs.

I don't want to engage in this conversation. "What can I do for you, Danny?"

He narrows his eyes. "Hey, how are you feeling after the accident? Healed yet?"

"Yes. Thank you. I'm almost a 100%."

"Good, good."

I don't believe for a second Danny is here to ask about my health status. And if not, then why the fuck is Danny paying me a visit today?

"What's up, Danny?" I get up from my chair and take a few steps forward. "Want anything to drink?"

"Oh, no, no," he says. "It'd be nice to chill by the pool, but that's not why I'm here."

"Okay."

"I'm here because we received an anonymous call

yesterday afternoon. It's about Jimmy. He's been reported missing."

A high-pitched ringing echoes in my ears and my vision blurs as my stomach turns itself inside out. My mind breaks into a million pieces, but I must keep my composure steady. At least I can still show some of the shock.

"Missing?" I repeat, widening my eyes.

"Yes. Missing. The caller said Jimmy often comes and goes, but he always comes home. It's never been this long since he hasn't returned. Plus, the person tried to call and never gets a return call." He shrugs his shoulders as if he's telling me a story with a great twist. "I guess they thought it was very unusual for Jimmy."

In my mind, I quickly recount all the people who might have placed that call. Who the hell could it be? Rose? Rose was awfully suspicious yesterday and kept asking about Jimmy. There was something in her demeanor that tells me she has questioned things. Besides, Rose has had a certain level of admiration for Jimmy; she has called him 'son' on many occasions. I wouldn't be surprised she called the cops out of concern for him. Considering how nosy she is, she'd easily notice his absence.

I shake my head to dislodge the thoughts of someone in my social circle being a snake. It can't be happening. It shouldn't.

If it isn't Rose, who else could it be? Skull? I've paid my pal to keep his mouth shut, and he'd have too much to lose. He'd be in just as deep shit as me if the truth came out. Besides, he's a true professional.

The only likely person I can think of is Lucy. She'd been so disappointed that Jimmy hasn't responded to her calls, texts, or the party invitation. But she's never met him before. She wouldn't know about his disappearing habits. No, no. It can't be Lucy.

"I don't know what to tell ya, Danny. I've already told you he comes and goes, but since I've moved in here, we have spoken a little as of late."

He nods as he watches me. "Yeah, I hear ya. I mean, you guys are separated or something, right?"

I don't know where he'd hear that from, but Hampton is a small town, so I wouldn't be surprised if someone at Red Urchin spread the news. Relief washes over me when I hear Danny's words, to which I only say, "Yes."

"Tell ya what." Danny gazes at the ocean. "If you hear from him, will you call me?"

"Of course, of course. I'd be more than happy to," I say. "But honestly, I don't have any desire to hear from him, nor do I expect it. We've mainly communicated through my lawyer."

I flinch as soon as I say that. Lawyer? We don't have a lawyer, and we're not getting divorced. I got myself stuck in this situation.

"I understand. But you never know. People sometimes become nicer out of guilt. Maybe he'll come around and apologize for whatever he's done to you."

I place my gaze on the ground. "Maybe."

He shrugs his shoulders. "If the only way to communicate with James is through your lawyer, I think it would be best if you give me his or her contact information. Can you give me the name?"

My blood freezes. How the hell do I get out of this situation? Do I make up the name?

"And also, it would be good if you gave me the phone number where I can reach them." He gives a quick nod, his eyebrows stitched together. That last sentence sounds more like an order than a polite request.

I must think on my feet. The only lawyer I've ever come across is Sam, who helped me redeem the lottery ticket. If I gave Danny her phone number, and he calls her, nothing will make any sense to either him or her. I need to come up with a better plan.

Then a thought hits me like a thunderbolt. "His name is Andrew."

"Andrew?"

He's the private investigator I hired when I suspected Jimmy wanted me killed and that he'd hired someone to follow me around. After our second meeting, he'd ghosted me, his phone number disconnected. I can give Danny that disconnected phone number. It will bide me some time until I figure out what the fuck to do next.

"Does he have a last name? Phone number?"

"His last name is Lawson. And here's the phone number."

I spell it out for him, controlling my shaky hands the best I can. Danny takes a small notepad out of his shirt pocket and a pen, jotting down what I just told him. His gaze goes back and forth between my face and the notepad, studying me carefully.

"Alright. Thanks for the phone number. I'll call him as soon as possible and see if we can trace your husband."

"You do that." I say. "But Andrew doesn't work on Sundays. I've called him multiple times on Sundays, and he's never responded. Just so you know."

"No worries. I wasn't planning on calling him today, anyway."

Relief washes over me. I'm really playing a dangerous game here, but hope makes me believe there's a way out.

We stand there for a few more seconds until Danny snaps out of it. "Well, I'll be out of your hair now. Take care."

He trudges across the front lawn, his hands resting on his hips. I turn around and look at the windows to find traces of Lucy. Did she see the cop outside? And if she did, would she ever suspect why he came over?

I'VE ALWAYS HATED SUNDAYS. There's a sense of foreboding nostalgia in them, something that pulls me into depression and bad feelings. Hanging out with Mom is such a drag. We have nothing to talk about, even though there are vast possibilities. We could talk about so many topics—we could discuss our favorite memories, share stories about our day, and sometimes dive into dreams for the future—but we both remain in our own world of silence. And most times, I don't want to start a conversation. Maybe because I'm afraid I'll learn more strange things about Lynn's life besides her drug addiction.

Instead of hanging by the pool with Lynn, I am in my room, lying on the bed, and contemplating my life since I've met her. Her presence only makes me miss Mary that much more. Sundays with Mary were so much more exciting, filled with laughter and joy. Every Sunday, she'd come up with a new recipe, and she and I'd hovered in the kitchen, making new food, like a great team we were.

Nothing like that has happened with Lynn yet. We don't have much in common, and she doesn't think of things for us to do on weekends. Not since our pedicures.

Lying in bed gets too old, so I get up to look out the window. An unusual sight outside catches my eye, and I remain put to see what the movement is about.

Across the front yard, a cop is surveying our house and yard. What's he doing here? Is it what I'm thinking it could be? Does it have something to do with the party yesterday? Did someone perhaps complain the music was loud? Is Lynn in trouble? Or am I?

Terror washes over me as I think of this possibility. I stand at the periphery of the window, hiding, and watching the cop advancing toward our house. He got in freely through the gate, which seems to have been unlocked because of Lynn's carelessness. I've locked it behind her way too many times and I'm a little tired of repeating myself that she must remember to lock it.

Now we have a cop walking in our yard, and things could get interesting.

I head for the door and downstairs and park myself at the window in the living room. I can see the cop and Lynn clearly, a sight that's confusing and puzzling at once. The cop is standing in front of Lynn, his hands resting on his hips. He's talking, but I can't hear a word he's saying, and I'm hating it. Lynn gets up and makes tentative steps toward him, holding onto the opal necklace she hasn't removed from her neck yet.

She looks flustered as she speaks. Her eyes are

enlarged as she taps her fingers on her neck. Her hand moves to her nose, and she scratches it twice. A typical sign of a liar. But what's she saying? What are they talking about?

The suspense is killing me. I watch the interaction unfold, wondering if I should join in and see what the visit is all about. But I retrieve and stay put. The cop takes a pad out of his shirt pocket and jots something down. Lynn is combing her hair with her fingers. I can tell she's nervous. But why?

A few minutes later, the cop turns around and walks away. Lynn, still standing in the same spot, clenches her hand into a fist and punches the palm of the other hand. All of this is a gigantic puzzle.

I make my way to the patio, finding Lynn staring at the ocean.

"Hey, Mom."

She turns around, sporting a fake smile. "Hi."

"What's the cop doing here?"

"Oh," she says, diverting her gaze away from me. "The cop? He was visiting to ask how I was doing. You know I was in a car accident a couple of months ago?"

"A car accident?" I hate how she tells me bits and pieces of news that I should have known all along.

Like a ghostly apparition, a chilling memory resurfaces in the recesses of my mind.

All night long, I remember following Jimmy in his car. He'd traversed the town, stopping at various locations, then abruptly reversed his car and sped away, continuing to the next destination. There was no doubt he was seeking something specific. He drove all night, with me following behind him at a safe distance, until he had to pull over at a gas station to replenish his tank.

He drove all around the town at a manic speed, checking every nook and cranny. I'd been curious about how much longer I could match his energy, but this mission was becoming exhausting, even for someone who stayed up all night gaming. My eyelids were getting droopy, and I was losing focus while driving.

But sometime around dusk, his lucky stars illuminated him.

He found Lynn's car.

He pulled into a hotel parking lot close to Lynn's car, then stormed out of his vehicle, clutching a toolbox. Jimmy was ready with a flashlight despite the dim overhead lights. As he slid underneath Lynn's car, a beam of light projected from beneath. His feet were poking out.

Despite my confusion about what I was seeing, I sat in my car, captivated by the sunrise, and waited for Jimmy to complete his task. Ten minutes later, Jimmy emerged from beneath the car, hurried to his vehicle, and sped off. What on earth was he doing? Was he involved in Lynn's accident in any way?

"Yeah. It was bad. My car got totaled," Lynn says.

"Oh, my God, Mom. How did it happen?"

"Well." Her eyes dart all over as she comes up with an answer. Then she shrugs her shoulders. "I wish I knew. I somehow lost control of the wheel and the next thing you know, I've collided with another car."

"Was something wrong with your car?"

"No. No." She shakes her head. "It just happened." Then she shrugs her shoulders again.

"So, the cop came to ask how you're doing after your car accident?"

"Yeah. Can you believe it? I've known him for a long time, plus he was the one who made appearance at the scene."

"That's awfully nice of him," I say. "But are you okay now? Does anything hurt?"

If it does, she never complained about it.

"No. I'm good. I really am," she says. She sounds convincing even though she looked like she was definitely hiding something when she talked to the cop. "I should probably go take a shower."

She turns on her heels and heads for the back kitchen door. She rushes up the stairs before disappearing into her bedroom.

And for the rest of the night, I don't see Lynn at all.

THE SOUND of footsteps outside my door wakes me up at daybreak.

The steps are not light. The feet stomp, seeking direction. Then I hear the dragging across the tile floor. What the hell is going on? Before I can get out of bed to find out, my bedroom door opens, and Lynn, her hair disheveled, face half-sleepy, walks through the door.

I sit up in bed, rubbing my eyes. Lynn is standing in the middle of my room, looking unsure about what to say. Perhaps there's an urgent matter to attend. Is she experiencing a heart attack? Maybe she needs me to drive her to the emergency room? Or maybe she's facing a midlife crisis?

However, as I become more accustomed to the surroundings, I realize Lynn isn't in her pajamas, despite the very early hour. She's fully dressed—denim jeans and a pink crop shirt—and ready to go somewhere. If she had time to put on bright red lipstick, then it's unlikely that she needs to be driven to the emergency room.

"Hi, love," she says. "Get ready. We're going to Paris!" She's trying to inject excitement into her voice, but it still sounds flat.

"What?" I rub my eyes again, as if that will make things clearer.

"I bought us plane tickets, and we're going to Paris. Today." She nods, unsure of herself, and of this whole interchange.

I look around, ensuring I'm not in some dream world. "Mom, what time is it?"

She takes the phone out of her back pocket and lights it up. "It's five a.m. Our flight is leaving at eight."

"Seriously? Why didn't you tell me about this earlier?"

"Well, I wanted it to be a delightful surprise." She grins, as a nervous laughter comes across her lips.

So many things could go wrong with this. She didn't even bother asking if I had a valid passport. Lucky for her, I do. When I was in high school, my parents sent me to Germany with it as an exchange student over the summer.

Reluctantly, I swing to the side of my bed and stand up. Outside of my bedroom door, I see a single bag sitting on the floor. It looks like Lynn has already packed all her stuff. "What about my job?" I ask.

Of course, I don't have a job, but at that moment, the question comes like a necessary distraction to this craziness. I want to know Lynn's thinking here; does she believe she can just sign me up for a trip without thinking of consequences?

"Oh, that. I'd booked our trip way before you told me about your job. Sorry about that. I was hoping you could just call them and ask them to postpone the start date."

I scoff and let out a big sigh. "Yeah, okay. I mean, I don't have a choice at this point. And I also have to pack quickly. I don't feel prepared."

"Don't worry about that. I was thinking maybe you can do all your shopping in Paris. Wouldn't that be fun?" Her eyes glisten.

It's not the worst thing that could happen, I guess. I can just stuff my purse with my wallet and toothbrush. In fact, a little shopping in Paris will be fun.

Lynn tilts her head and scrunches up her face in remorse. "I'm so sorry, Lucy. I really wanted to do something special for you ... for us."

In an instant, I'm ridden with guilt. Lynn's only intention was to make me happy. For crying out loud, she's taking me to a place I've always wanted to visit. All the cafes and restaurants. I'm always intrigued to see how people live there. Now, it's becoming a reality. I've only ever seen pictures. When Rebecca went a couple of years ago, she kept posting all her pictures on Instagram.

Hashtag Paris.

Hashtag De Louvre.

Hashtag Notre Dame.

I was filled with envy and wished with all my might to be that irritating person one day.

I approach Lynn and give her a bear hug. "Thanks, Mom. I really appreciate it."

She puts her arms around me and squeezes me lightly, then pulls away.

"I'm looking forward to spending quality time with you and getting to know you better."

Now I see what this is all about. However, she must remember that it's a two-way street. This is a great opportunity to get closer to Lynn and ask her the pressing questions. Like things about my biological dad. I'm so curious about how their marriage is suddenly dissolving when they could be happy together with all this wealth. They could go on this trip now. They could enjoy life outside the little world they have built together.

But I won't complain. I'll take every opportunity Lynn presents to see the world.

Still half-asleep, I trudge to the bathroom to brush my teeth and pack up all my essentials. On my way out, I put a few things in my purse and get dressed. I could use coffee, but, according to Lynn, we're running out of time. Our Uber ride should be here any minute.

"We can get coffee at the airport," she adds.

While I'm ascending the steps, half-asleep, putting half of my weight on the railing, Lynn frantically stomps down the steps, dragging the luggage behind her, and the noise echoes through the house. Something in her disposition seems wrong. I sense little excitement over our quest to spend quality time together. And if my hunch is correct, then I wonder what prompted Lynn to come up with this plan.

DANNY'S VISIT has shaken me to my core.

I'm struggling with the fact that Jimmy has been officially listed as missing. But what did I expect? Eventually, someone would notice he was missing and question it. I'm still pondering over the potential people who might have reported to the cops. Jimmy quit his job before I killed him, so it couldn't have been his employer. That bridge was burned long ago.

The only true suspect in my mind is Rose, as she was accustomed to seeing Jimmy all the time, and suddenly he was gone. Plus, she was asking too many questions at the party.

Often, I've wondered: should I just confess and turn myself into the police? Tell them the entire story about how Jimmy used to beat me, and how, just before I killed him, he tampered with my car brakes that led to an accident. I nearly died. The difficulty lies in the fact that I had no way to prove Jimmy's involvement in my car brake incident. Danny is convinced that it was rats who caused damage to my car. How could I argue with him? It's a no-win game.

For now, I'm happy I'm about to hop on a plane to Paris with Lucy and spend a week away. This will be a great opportunity, not just to connect more deeply with her, but also to devise my next steps.

Last night, as soon as Danny left, I bought two plane tickets. My passport is in my safe. After I killed Jimmy, I had a foresight that I might need to get away far, at least temporarily, so I had a passport issued. I've never traveled outside of New England. I've never been farther than Rhode Island. And that was many years ago when Jimmy took me to a concert of a local band. We got there and spent a night in Providence. I'd thought he would take me out to brunch and talk about our lovely experience from the previous night. But no. The following morning, we returned home and never talked about our trip again.

Paris, I've heard, is a grand place. I deceived Lucy by claiming this was part of a long-standing plan, but I can't disclose my urgency to escape Hampton.

All I want is to clear my head.

Lucy is standing in the hallway, still half asleep, her purse on her shoulder. She's smiling. "I'm ready."

"You look beautiful."

She gives me a smile of an angel before we realize we're frozen in place, staring at each other. Lucy's eyes are watery and heavy, and I sense innocence in them. If she only knew what I've done, would she forgive me? I'm taking her away from a job that she was excited about. Sure, I could go to Paris alone, but I fear Danny might pay a visit to the house again, then Lucy might find out what's going on.

We snap out of our staring contest and head downstairs. An Uber driver is parked just outside of our gate, waiting for us. We lock the gate behind us and enter the car, relieved we're moving on to the next destination—the airport. The driver is moving too slowly, shedding every nerve in my body. The news is on the radio, and I tense up as I think about Lucy listening to an announcement that a local man, James Corrigan, is missing, and that if anyone has any information, they should call the local Hampton police.

"I'm sorry, but can you turn down the radio? I'm just not in the mood to listen."

The driver gives me a look through the mirror and reaches for the volume dial. Lucy looks at me with concern on her face. "Are you okay?"

Still rattled, I tell her I'm fine. Just too tired and excited to be listening to the news this early in the morning.

I sigh with relief when the driver drops us off at the airport. We enter the vast building, and anxiety rises inside me. Lucy stirs me in the right direction and tells me to follow her, perhaps guessing this is my first time at the airport. People hurry towards me, their shoulders brushing mine, as I try to keep up with Lucy. We go through the customs, then head to our gate where the sign that says Paris flight is on time sparkles from a distance.

As we wait for our flight to board, both Lucy and I engross ourselves in our respective phones, allowing silence to settle between us. My fingers frantically search for news on Jimmy. I type in his name and click on the search button, and there it is. A missing person report on some obscure website with tons of ads flashing. I glance at Lucy to make sure she didn't see me, but she is still staring at her phone, typing away.

Shit. This makes me nervous, but then, what are the odds of Lucy discovering this article? I suspect she won't be searching for it, and I don't see her coming across it randomly.

I'm thinking too much. I just need to relax for once.

As saved by the bell, the voice behind a speaker finally calls for those boarding our plane. We stroll toward the gate, and I feel as if we're going to a torture chamber rather than one of the most beautiful cities on Earth.

CHAPTER 28

LUCY

BEFORE WE HOP on the plane, I debate whether I should let Evan know I'm going to Paris. I'm not obligated to inform him about my whereabouts, but this trip is abrupt and may raise some concerns for him. After all, we hung out at his place at least twice a week, so if I'm gone for an entire week, he'll wonder why I haven't stopped by. It would be the right thing to do.

But something tells me not to. That nagging voice advises me to keep things to myself, even though he might worry about me. Plus, I don't want to lead Evan on, thinking constant check-ins may become the norm between us. It won't.

As we board the plane, the flight attendant greets us and checks our tickets. Lynn's eyes bulge like she's just seen a ghost. I can tell she fears flying, so I put my hand on her shoulder and gently caress it. "Mom, you'll be okay."

As we both proceed to the heart of the plane, the attendant calls Lynn and says, "Excuse me, ma'am."

Lynn turns around, her face etched in fear. All the color has drained from her face. She bites her bottom lip and clutches her purse tightly.

"Yes ... yes?" she stumbles on her words.

The flight attendant glares as we hinder other passengers from entering the plane, slowing down the process. "You have a ticket for first class."

"What?" I exclaim.

I can't believe she booked a first-class ticket for herself and a coach ticket for me. With the amount of money she has, you'd think she could afford to buy both of us a first-class ticket.

"I ... I don't understand," Lynn says.

Lynn looks genuinely confused, as if she doesn't know how this mishap happened. I know how—Lynn is simply clueless about life.

"Please proceed this way." The flight attendant extends her arm toward the front side of the plane.

Lynn looks at me with remorse on her face. "Do you want my seat?"

She's clearly so full of guilt that she wants to do everything right by me. Appeasing me is her main goal.

"Sure."

"Okay." She nods, looking relieved.

We swap our boarding passes, so we know our new respective seats. Saying nothing further, I turn around and walk toward first class, where luxury awaits. As soon as I find my seat, a flight attendant patrols around, asking if I need anything. She's holding a tray of bubbly drinks and a small plate full of olives. My seat is giant compared to what I've seen on planes before, and I pinch myself to ensure it's real. This ride sure promises to be comfortable.

As soon as the plane ascends into the air, my mind wanders. Now I have time to think, there are a whole six hours of nothing but roaring engines and white skies outside the window. Evan comes to mind. Memories from when we first met. I think back to when Mary died, and how Fred grieved her as much as I had, but he moved on much more quickly than I did.

I didn't turn to Fred for comfort; instead, I sought out a support group for those who have lost loved ones. You'd be surprised how many groups there were out there. Losing loved ones and dealing with the pain they leave behind is a struggle experienced by everyone. One minute we are here. The next, we're gone forever.

The group had been meeting for a while, and when I joined, I felt isolated, like a lone wolf in a forest. The physical appearance of the place didn't make me feel any better. Located in the industrial part of Hampton, the building had established small businesses on each floor. The room we met in was a six-hundred square foot space, empty except for plastic chairs circled around. The carpet, which hadn't been washed for years, appeared overused and gray. Against a wall, was a long table with Dunkin Donuts boxed coffee and munchkins. We all took turns to bring those in, even though I rarely partook in eating.

The first time I attended, the group leader asked me to introduce myself and tell my story, and timidly, I told them how my mother, Mary, dropped dead of a heart attack in our very own kitchen. She'd be lying lifeless for a few hours when I walked in and found her. I hated seeing her dead body like that, her eyes staring at the ceiling, the whites of her eyes matching the color of her skin.

Everyone stared at me as I spoke. They all had stories of their own, some heavier and sadder than mine. They all had shared their history, and their pasts glued us together. A universal understanding of loss bonded us.

I went outside for a break one day to light a blunt, hiding from my new support family. At least, in that instance, they felt like a family. The kind where you find your own pack, but still hide your true identity.

I was hiding behind the building when Evan's voice startled me. "Hey."

"Hey." I looked at him with annoyance. He'd caught me smoking weed behind the building, something I was never proud of. It was a bad habit I'd developed over years, my way to relax and keep the problems at bay; forget the shit that lingered on my mind.

"I'm Evan. Nice to meet you." He smiled.

"I know your name. I've heard you speak inside." I avoided his intense gaze.

"I'm sorry about your mom."

I nodded, then turned to face him. He sounded genuine. "Thanks." I inhaled and exhaled a puff, then looked at him. "It's been a few years since she died, but I still miss her."

He nodded. "I understand. It's hard to lose a parent."

"Sorry about your son. That must be tough."

His eyes teared up instantly, but he snapped out of it, stifling the reaction. "Yeah, it is. I miss him. I miss him so much." He looked down and wiped the tear from his eye.

I didn't know what to say about that. It sounded it like he might have lost his son forever, even though he was still among the living. I didn't know what was worse: losing a person to heaven or to ill circumstances.

Instead, I offered my blunt, and to my relief he took it, dragging a big puff then releasing the smoke into the air. We looked at each other for a minute, then he said, "Hey, I think I know you from somewhere." He squinted to take a better look at me.

"Oh, yeah? From where? I don't live around here. I drive from Conway for these meetings."

I traveled two hours each way to Hampton, where the support group was held, in the hopes of running into Jimmy. I had nothing better to do than find ways to increase my chances of seeing him.

Evan shrugged his shoulders. "You just look so familiar. I can't put my finger on it."

I shrugged too, unable to demystify his conundrum. I'd been hanging around Hampton and following Jimmy around. It was quite possible he'd seen me, working hard at staying incognito. I didn't want to tell him, but I was confident that I'd spotted him somewhere else too, before these support group sessions.

———

As my thoughts carry me to sleep, the flight attendant comes by and offers a snack of mixed nuts and a glass of orange juice. I shake my head slightly and thank her. I'm not hungry or thirsty.

I put my seat down and close my eyes, hoping to fall asleep, but sleep doesn't come. What comes to mind is Lynn. My mother. My biological mother.

Now that we've embarked on this trip, far away from home, we can delve deeper into our own pasts. I'm dying to learn more about her, about James—or as everyone calls him, Jimmy. I'm awfully curious about what led to the downward spiral of their marriage. Of course, I know he used to beat her. I know he was a terrible son of a gun to her and that she just took it with no self-defense.

I know all this because I stalked Jimmy for the longest time. I watched fights and beatings unfold in the house, in front of my own eyes. Jimmy grabbing Lynn by the scruff of her neck, then plastering her into the wall. She'd then fall helpless on the floor. I couldn't tell from a distance if she sobbed, but I imagine she did. Domestic abuse brings physical and emotional pain.

Jimmy's beating of his wife helped me understood why he wanted nothing to do with me. With our nuclear family. Him, Lynn, and I. God, what a fucking disaster that would be.

I'm curious when I press Lynn. Will she open up to me and tell me the truth? Will she tell me Jimmy beat her?

Isn't trust built on truth?

I can't help but wonder if she'll tell me the other stuff. Like the fact that I have two half-sisters, born to the same father.

She probably thinks I don't know. And I bet she'd never suspect her daughter is an expert stalker.

MY OBSESSION with stalking Jimmy had intensified over time.

I dropped out of college because of it. At first, I'd skip the last two lectures of the day and head east to Hampton to look for him. It was a lot more interesting to watch my biological father do things from a distance than learn about marketing schemes and what-not. I became so obsessed that, instead of caring to finish college and get a good job after, all I cared about was to follow Jimmy around, find out what he'd been up to, what life choices he'd made regarding everyday life.

Whom else he'd rejected.

It was bound to happen one day.

I followed Jimmy on a windy day, having skipped school. I didn't feel like going to classes, so I decided I'd take a ride to Hampton and see what my other dad was up to that day. He left the auto shop, looking agitated as he entered his car before taking off at a mad speed. I almost lost him as I trailed his car. He parked a block from the beach, hopped out of his car, and urgently walked to a woman standing on the curb, looking at the ocean. He must have said something, causing her to turn around and face him. There appeared to be no niceties or pleasant exchanges.

They were having a heated discussion. Jimmy was gesticulating with his hands while she looked at him defiantly.

I watched them from a safe distance. Jimmy kept shouting, getting closer to her face, while she was crying. I couldn't hear his voice, but I could see his face contorted into rage. They stood there, having a conversation, or rather, Jimmy having a monologue, when suddenly, Jimmy lifted his hand and swung it toward the woman's face, slapping it hard. She instinctively grabbed her cheek, her eyes growing wide, her mouth agape at the shock of Jimmy's strike. I flinched at the scene and put my hand on my own cheek, as if feeling the burn. Jimmy said something else, then turned around and walked away. The young woman stood there, stunned, and wiped tears from her face.

I jumped out of my car and headed in the woman's direction, careful not to scare her off.

"Excuse me," I said. "I just noticed you talking to that man."

Her watery eyes peered closely at me, as if she was unsure of what I wanted from her.

"He's my father," I blurted out. She looked at me with wide eyes, etched with surprise, relief, disbelief all at once.

"Mine, too. Unfortunately." She laughed through tears.

She looked a spitting image of Jimmy: intense blue eyes, a chin dimple, and lush hair most of us would die for. There was no question she was his daughter.

"I didn't know I had a half-sister until now." I took her hand in mine and smiled.

She squeezed mine lightly. "Now there're three of us. At least that I know of."

"Three?" it was my turn to be in shock.

"Jimmy has three daughters he wants nothing to do with. I'm the eldest."

Jimmy's rejection stung only a little less.

"What's your name?" I asked her.

"Cheryl." She gave a nod. "But I don't live around here. I came here, hoping to meet Jimmy. Didn't pan out as I'd hoped."

That was the last time I saw Cheryl. But at least I knew a bit of the history of Jimmy's extramarital affairs and his habit of bringing unwanted children into the world. Given the suffering he'd inflicted upon us, I couldn't help but feel conflicting emotions towards him. One of them being close to hatred.

———

By the time the plane descends on the runway, the city is already wrapped in the darkness. Paris sparkles in all its glory and I can see the Eiffel Tower from my plane window. Only then do I feel excitement tingling in my belly. I've always wanted to visit the city, but it was out of reach, mainly because I've been broke all my life.

I find Lynn standing at the gate, looking nervous. When she sees me, she spreads her arms wide for a hug. "Oh, Lucy, I thought you'd never come out."

I approach and give her a hug, smelling the heavy scent of her sweat.

"I have no other place to go," I tell her. "This is the only way out."

Lynn is a hot mess. She always appears so nervous, looking over her shoulder, clinging to me for reassurances. She wants to know she's fine. It's almost as if she's afraid of losing me again. But I do my best to let her know I'm here to stay. I won't be going anywhere.

We claim Lynn's baggage and exit the airport, looking for transportation to our hotel. Lynn takes a piece of paper out of her purse and reads from it.

"Our hotel is in the heart of the city. Here." She hands me the piece of paper.

Judging from the picture of the room and its exterior, it promises a comfortable stay. We hail a cab and tell the driver to get us there. As we ride through a dark neighborhood, Lynn and I stare out of the window, mesmerized by the city. I can't wait to explore it, and I'm looking forward to getting to know my mom better. I hope she'll find this new, beautiful environment invigorating and she can finally relax a little. Not think of Jimmy. Her divorce. Everything she has gone through in her life. Not that you can suddenly escape it so easily. But maybe, just for a week, she can have quality time in the City of Light.

Lynn takes my hand and squeezes it. I turn around and the light reflection from the outside brighten up her face. Her lips morph into a small smile, and I'm relieved to see her happy.

At the hotel, we check in, then take the elevator up to our room. Lynn booked a suite on the top floor. The room is stunning. It's spacious, featuring tasteful furniture and décor that takes our breath away. There are two separate rooms with a single bed, one for each of us. In the middle is a bathroom with two sinks, a large tub and a standing shower. Around the edge of the main room is a seating area with a couch, two chairs, and coffee table. The kitchenette in the corner has all the essentials plus a coffee maker.

All seems wonderful, but there won't be any space to escape to when I need a break from Lynn.

She comes over to the tall windows and opens the curtains. Across the way stands a building etched in intricate architectural details, and below is a coffee shop with a patio outside. French living at its finest. We are taking it all in, inhaling and exhaling deeply, but I feel exhausted, and I tell Lynn I want to hit the sack and rest my eyes a bit. It's already late here, with the six-hour time difference.

She ignores my quest for rest and takes the phone out of her pocket. She looks at it for a while and her face contorts into a confused frown. Her eyes meet mine, then she says, "My phone isn't working."

"Yeah, you're in a different country now. You either need to buy international data or get Wi-Fi to connect."

She's still looking at me, puzzled, as if I was speaking ancient Greek. It's just another sign of how uncultured and inexperienced Lynn is, and part of me feels bad for her. Being married to Jimmy, who never took her anywhere at all, has clearly affected her ability to adapt in an ever-changing world.

"So, what should I do? I can't use it at all?"

"I'm sure the hotel has Wi-Fi. We can ask for it later. I'm super tired and need to sleep." Waking up at five isn't a common theme in my life. Although my plane seat was beyond comfortable, I can never sleep on a plane.

"You know what? How about I leave the phone in my purse and not use it for the entire week?" She nods, pride coming out of her eyes. I don't tell her that to survive in a big city, one of us needs a phone to search for places, or to use google maps to find our way around. If I were to choose between the two of us, it better be me.

"Okay, Mom. That sounds good." I give her a quick hug and turn around to walk to my bed. As soon as I hit the pillow, I'm in dreamland.

But sometime early in the morning, it must be around two or three a.m., Lynn's voice wakes me up. It's muffled by the wall between us—she sounds like she's talking from the bottom of a deep barrel. I prop myself up to make sense of what she's saying. Still uncertain, I get up and come closer to the wall, placing my ear against the cold, white wallpaper.

"Jimmy. Please. No. Jimmy." She then wails and howls like an animal. As I listen to her howls, I'm rooted to my spot, frozen. "Jimmy. Jimmy. Forgive me."

Her words make me flinch, not just the noise.

I don't know what to do. Wake her up? There's no doubt that she's having nightmares, and the howls, growls, and calling for Jimmy are making it impossible for me to sleep. I don't want to listen to Lynn. Instead of waking her up, I remain in my spot and wait.

She continues making sounds for a minute or two longer, then they halt. I go back to my bed, pondering what demons Lynn carries.

I hope to find out soon.

CHAPTER 30

LYNN

I WAKE up as the gentle morning light seeps through the curtains of our Parisian apartment. The coffee aroma wafts through the air, prompting my eyes to flutter open. The alluring fragrance directs me to a charming corner of the kitchen, promising a delightful new day. There, Lucy, my daughter and newfound companion in this adventure, stands with a welcoming smile. As I inhale the familiar scent, I feel the allure of Paris awakening not just my surroundings but a sudden sense of joy within me.

But there's also a terrible sense of dread buried deep inside of me.

Lucy glances over her shoulder and greets me with a singsong voice. "Hi, Mom. How did you sleep?"

Although I slept poorly, I don't want to dampen the mood. It might be the new bed or the six-hour time difference between Hampton and Paris. I've heard of jet lag before, but this is my first encounter with it. "I slept well. How about you?"

"Great!" she exclaims. "I'm excited to be here." Turning to face me, she adds, "I woke up early to plan all the activities for our trip. Today, we're going to explore Notre Dame and a couple of museums. And I need to do some clothes shopping, too."

"That sounds wonderful," I reply, willing to go along with whatever Lucy proposes. After sipping our coffee in silence, I contemplate the day ahead. Glancing at the clock, I realize it's already ten. How did I sleep so late?

Lucy announces she's going to take a quick shower, and then we can head out. As I mull over my thoughts, Danny's image intrudes—Jimmy reported missing, Danny investigating—all the mysteries swirling in my mind.

It feels like an inescapable bad dream.

Lucy emerges from the bathroom with a towel wrapped around her head. "Let me dry my hair a bit, and I'll be ready to go."

I stand up and drag myself to my corner of the suite to change into decent clothes, brush my teeth, and fix my hair. While the excitement of being in Paris invigorated Lucy, I can't muster the same enthusiasm. I just want to escape the mess at home, even if only for a short while. I'm finding it impossible to plan my next steps, but maybe this trip will bring some clarity.

We head down to the lobby, which looks different in the daylight. Only then do I notice a bar section where people are enjoying early mimosas. We opt for the dining area to grab breakfast since we plan to walk all day.

Mine and Lucy's first day in Paris consists of

wandering the streets and indulging in shopping. She buys an abundance of clothes, barely trying them on. While we embrace the Paris experience, I observe locals speaking softly with great politeness. I don't know why, but Barbara's harsh voice comes to mind as I think of people back home. What a difference. In contrast to my hometown, there's no impatient honking from cars on the streets of Paris. Like us, the tourists wander around, amazed and awestruck by the sights. It feels like a different world.

On days two and three, Lucy and I embark on yet another enchanting journey, weaving through the Paris cobblestone streets, which are adorned with the whispers of history. The Eiffel Tower looms majestically, a timeless symbol of romance, as we stroll along the Seine, the river mirroring the city's allure. In quaint bistros, we savor the delicate flavors of French cuisine, each bite a celebration of our newfound bond. The Louvre beckons, its grandeur overwhelming yet inviting, while housing the echoes of artistic brilliance through the ages. As nightfall drapes the city in a soft glow, we ascend to Montmartre, where the city sprawls beneath us like a canvas painted with dreams. Paris unfolds before us, a tapestry of culture and love, leaving us with indelible memories etched into our shared history.

But day four brings a completely different vibe.

As soon we step outside our hotel, an inexplicable sense of dread washes over me. People stroll by, appearing calm and happy—a stark contrast to my current state. I'm tempted to go back to our room for safety, but Lucy's voice is alluring.

"Let's go this way," Lucy directs, consulting her phone to map our route. "If we walk by the river, we'll hit all the major tourist attractions."

I follow behind her, shuffling my feet, unsure of myself. I wish I could match Lucy's excitement, but I'm mentally and emotionally spent. For one, I'm worried sick about what has transpired since Sunday, the day Danny came to visit. Did he call Andrew? If he did, what did he think about reaching the disconnected number? It would all seem so suspicious. Did he come back to my house to instigate further? What did he think when he found it empty?

Dizziness hits me as these thoughts run though my head. Haven't I gotten myself into more trouble by running away?

As we stroll down the streets, the city views become even more beautiful, but nothing lifts my spirits.

Several blocks from our hotel, Lucy asks about stopping by some boutiques on our way back. Everything looks expensive, but in her rush to catch our flight, she didn't pack clothes, and I *had* promised to take her shopping. Clearly, the vast array she's already bought today hasn't been enough to satisfy her. Her eyes gleam with enthusiasm when she stares at the store window, longing for high-end fashionable items.

As we stand at the store window, something catches my eye, and I pause for a moment to observe. A male mannequin eerily resembling Jimmy triggers a shiver of fear.

He haunts me everywhere—dreams, thoughts, and now, even in Paris.

When I turn to catch up with Lucy, she's nowhere in sight. I call her name, but my voice doesn't reach far. I enter the store, presuming she might be on another shopping spree, but I don't see her there. I look to my left, then to my right, and Lucy hasn't emerged. She's nowhere to be found.

Panicking, and with no sense of direction, I realize I don't know how to get back to our hotel. Even on day four, the city appears as one confusing maze, and frustration mounts. A screech escapes me, tears well up, and all I want is to escape this nightmare.

I choose a direction, hoping to find our hotel, but the more I walk, the less familiar everything becomes. Panic sets in, my heart races, and my palms sweat. Every corner looks the same, and I curse my decision to be here.

I take my phone out of my purse, only to remember that it's useless. Why had I agreed to put it away while we're here? I've relied on Lucy to take us places and bring us back to the hotel, all in one piece. I'm suddenly wary of her intentions. Can I trust her? My one and only daughter who's abandoned me on the streets of Paris?

Bile rises my throat, and I'm one step away from throwing up, but I control it. Last thing I want to do is embarrass myself in front of the passersby.

Instead, out of nowhere, I scream. I'm overwhelmed

with emotion as I desperately scan my surroundings for a route to take.

Heading in what I believe is the direction of our hotel, the stores don't look familiar. Was I not paying attention? Lucy is still missing. Is she searching for me? Why would she care, though? I've provided her with money, and she doesn't need to worry. She's probably having fun shopping and exploring. My feet carry me deeper into the city, and I finally reach the river. This can't possibly be close to our hotel.

I'm lost. I'm so, so lost.

Approaching an elderly woman walking in the opposite direction, I desperately cut off her path. Startled, she tries to avoid me, but I grab her arm, pleading, "Help me. Please help me. I'm lost." For a moment, it crosses my mind that getting lost can't be a coincidence. The realization hits me.

Lucy might have orchestrated all of this.

I'M FEELING helpless and alone in my attempt to find my way back to the hotel. Paris isn't Hampton, the small ocean town where I've learned every nook and cranny over the decades of living there. The lady I've marked as my savior senses panic in me, so she stops and offers to help. She speaks broken English but understands me enough to converse.

"Please help me," I plead with her, tears welling up in my eyes.

"What you need?"

The look on her face is sympathetic. She emanates a quiet grace that seems to transcend the years. Her silver hair is neatly tied, and a pair of well-worn spectacles are perched on her nose, lending an air of wisdom to her gaze.

I clutch my purse, my stomach doing a thousand somersaults.

"I'm lost. I need to get to my hotel."

"Name hotel."

The woman is stoically patient, and she reminds me of my grandmother when she taught me to read at five. I don't know why she comes to mind now, but suddenly, I miss being back home as distant memories emerge.

"Europe."

She takes her phone out and locates it on the map. I come closer and hover over the phone to see how far I've walked. I'm shocked to see the hotel is less than a mile away. I must have walked in circles for a while, ultimately landing where I am, by the river. The woman points toward the hotel. "Dis way. Walk straight, then take the left. Two blocks hotel."

It's a straight shot to the hotel. I look at my watch and notice I've walked for several hours, wandering the streets of Paris. Where is Lucy? Is she having fun? If she knew I got lost and fell into the panic mode, would she be laughing? Well, shoot, anyone would have a laugh if they knew what a ditz I've been on this trip.

None of this feels right.

I trudge through the streets, and several blocks away, I see the familiar building standing in a corner. It's our hotel. The big sign EUROPE sits across the entrance door. I stop for a second and sigh in relief. It feels like I narrowly escaped death. Again.

The hotel looks busy, with people coming in and out. I walk in and sigh with relief when I see the familiar space. I glance at the bar, spotting people at the tables, eating late lunch. I do a double take when, at the periphery of my vision, I see the familiar-looking face. It's Lucy. She's sitting at a table, several fancy-looking paper bags spread on the floor next to her. She's reading a book and paying no attention to the world.

Anger rises inside me, but I quickly put my face in check. I can't show her how mad I really am. I unclench my fists and walk over to her. She's so deeply into her book she doesn't notice me at first. I clear my throat, and she lifts her head.

A smile spreads on her face. "Hi, Mom."

She hasn't even questioned where I've been the past two hours. My stomach churns.

"Hi," I say, unamused.

"What happened? Where did you go?"

Where did I go? Oh, how convenient for her to assume that I just took off.

"We must have separated somehow. Then I got lost."

She drops the book to the table, her brows stitching together in sympathy. "Oh, Mom. I'm so sorry. I just assumed you wanted to part ways and do your thing."

My nostrils flare up at her casual delivery. How can she be so obtuse? But I need to give her the benefit of the doubt. Lucy might not have done it on purpose. I inhale and exhale slowly and find my way to calm.

"Mom, sit down. Relax. Let's order something to eat."

I pull the chair out across from her and sit down. "Okay."

"I made a reservation for a restaurant tonight. You're going to love it. We'll need to dress up since it's fancy." She lets out a little laugh.

I usually like when she laughs, but I can't stand it now. I'm still trying to recover from the impact of my previous experience. I scoff, then clear my throat to conceal my cynicism. I'd rather stay in the room, curl up in bed, and sleep. But I can't say no to Lucy, can I?

"Sounds like a plan," I confirm.

I should hook my phone to the Wi-Fi, so I don't need to rely on following Lucy's lead on the trip anymore. Damn it, I should have done that as soon as we arrived, but trusting Lucy took precedence. I take my phone out of my purse and ask Lucy what the hotel's Wi-Fi passcode is. The second I'm connected, text messages pour in.

But one stands out.

It's from Skull. All in caps.

LYNN, WE GOTTA MEET UP.

I WATCH Lynn scroll through her phone, looking curious but not quite at ease. Her jaw slackens and her skin goes deathly pale. She throws me a stiff smile before putting the phone away.

She's hiding something.

"Is everything okay, Mom?"

She lifts her head suddenly and looks at me. Her face is white as a ghost, and she looks lost. "Yes. Everything's fine. I'm just tired after walking for hours."

"Should we go to our room? I'm tired as well. I could take a nap before dinner."

We get up in unison and take the elevator up to the suite.

When we enter our suite, we both retreat to our respective corners. I hit the sack and close my eyes. Will Lynn talk in her sleep again? I didn't tell Lynn that she's done it every night since we arrived, and nor do I intend to.

I don't want to delve into why she'd requested Jimmy's forgiveness in her sleep.

Minutes later, a muffled voice by the wall draws my full attention. "Shit, shit, shit." Lynn sounds upset. She's obviously talking to herself, and I'm dying to know what she's cussing about. I brush these thoughts aside and fall asleep.

It's dark when I wake up. The lights from the outside gently caress the objects in the room. I sit up on my bed and rub my eyes, forcing myself to fully wake up. The suite is peaceful, and there are no indications of Lynn's presence. She must be sleeping. A single honk echoes outside. I look at my watch and notice it's past seven already. Our reservation at the restaurant is at eight. Shit.

The door to Lynn's bedroom is wide open, and I peer inside, only to find it empty. Where could she be? Just as I'm about to head for the door and look for her in the lobby, the door opens, and Lynn walks through, looking frazzled.

"Hey, I've been looking for you."

Her eyes are enormous as she stares at me, then she says, "Oh. I had to make a quick phone call."

She turns her eyes away from me and strides across the room, her fingers combing through her hair.

"Is everything okay?" I call after her.

"Everything's fine."

It's hard to believe this, but I don't challenge her. She's been acting too strange today. Does it have anything to do with whatever she saw on her phone?

"Okay. If everything's fine, you should get ready for dinner." My voice carries through the suite.

I get no response.

Half an hour later, Lynn walks out of her room, dressed up to the nines. She's wearing a beautiful red dress, which delicately hugs her small curves, and a light white shawl across her shoulders. Her makeup is striking, making her look stunning. Her hair, once messy, is now combed to one side, beautifully enhancing her face.

I gasp. "Mom. Wow. You look so beautiful."

She tilts her head and gives me a small smile. "Thank you, so do you."

I've done my own pampering for this occasion and I'm wearing the dress I bought today. I look and feel like a million bucks.

We arrive at the restaurant a little after eight. The host walks us to our table. As we stride ahead, Lynn looks mesmerized by the restaurant's interior. The ambiance is a blend of rustic charm and Parisian sophistication, with vintage chandeliers casting a warm glow over weathered wooden tables adorned with crisp white linens. The air is infused with the aroma of culinary delights—rich sauces, freshly baked baguettes, and the luring smells of French herbs. Soft jazz notes waft from a corner, adding to the intimate atmosphere.

The architecture, the décor, the lighting. It's probably like nothing she's seen before. Her mouth is agape, and her eyes are wide as they dart all over the place.

We sit down, and Lynn looks at me, astounded. "This place is gorgeous."

I cup her hand with mine. "I'm so glad you like it. I've checked the place on Tripadvisor. It's one of the best restaurants in Paris."

Maybe the ambiance will relax her and give her some reprieve from life back home. For at least the duration of dinner.

But even with the comforting ambiance, Lynn looks unsettled, her eyes avoiding mine. She takes her glass of water every minute and sips from it, watching me from the edge of the glass rim. It's clear that she's thinking about something, but we're struggling to find a way to initiate a conversation and establish a connection.

"How do you like Paris?" I break the silence.

She nods quickly. "Good. Okay. It's okay."

"It's different, that's for sure."

She smiles and nods, taking her water glass. She has nearly emptied it, so a waiter approaches our table and refills the glass. While he's there, I order a bottle of red wine and two glasses. I'm fully aware Lynn doesn't drink alcohol, but this is a special occasion, and she could handle a glass or two.

He brings it promptly and pours it into one glass, expecting one of us to taste it. Lynn wants nothing to do with it, so I reach for the glass, take a sip, and then nod. "It's perfect."

The waiter smiles and pours both glasses before walking away.

French restaurants are slow at serving food. Fancy ones? Even slower. I have enough time to tame Lynn into a meaningful conversation. Before I even start, I put my glass in the air. "Cheers."

Lynn hesitates before taking her glass, but then follows my lead by holding up her wine and taking a sip. Because she's not a drinker, the alcohol will probably go straight to her head. After a couple of sips, her shoulders relax, and she looks me right in the eye, bolder and more confident. The waiter brings a basket of warm bread and butter, saying something in French, and Lynn lets out a giddy laugh. This is a new side of her that I haven't seen before, and I'm amused by it. I prefer her over the nervous and lost Lynn.

While we share bread, we exchange small talk about French food, and our plans for the next two days. Two more days, and we go back home.

As Lynn stares at me, a wide smile on her face, I find a perfect time to start my questions. It might be wishful thinking to expect my mother to disclose anything new about Jimmy, but I'm willing to give it a shot.

"So, Mom. I need to ask you about Jimmy."

Lynn's smile vanishes, and her mouth turns down at the corners.

"What about Jimmy?" she says.

"What's he like? I mean, I never really got to know him well, and I'm curious."

Her fingers lace together as she gives me a tentative

gaze, then drops her head down and looks at me with pain in her eyes.

"He was a good man."

I flinch at this statement. A good man? Based on everything she's endured from him throughout their marriage? I've observed numerous fights and beatings from a safe distance, and questioned why she hasn't managed to break free from the clutches of the monster.

"A good man?" I repeat.

She nods. "We have had our disagreements and differences, but he was loyal."

Loyal? He impregnated two other women, giving him two other daughters. She must have known this, right? Maybe we don't have the same definition of loyalty, but Jimmy was a cheating bastard, clearly hoping for a different woman to give him a son. That's what I was told, anyway.

"Did he ever ... you know, raise his hand on you?"

"What?" Lynn looks flustered, as if trying to process my question. "Oh, no. No, no." She averts her gaze away and chugs down her wine.

I want to throw up. Loyal? Jimmy never landing a hand on her? She's spewing lies at me, and with such ease, too. She tells me nothing about my stepsisters. It's difficult to believe she doesn't know about them. So much for building a trusting relationship with my own mother.

What's she trying to cover up?

I DON'T KNOW why Lucy is asking me all these questions about Jimmy, but they're making me uncomfortable. I can't wait to get out of here. Twenty minutes after Lucy started grilling me, our food finally arrives, and I'm grateful to focus on eating rather than this awful conversation.

With Lucy probing and poking into my past, I fear a whole can of worms will open. I'm afraid I'll reveal everything to her. I know exactly what she's up to: have another glass of wine, Mom, relax, and get carried away. She knows I'll somehow trust my companion in the heat of the moment and end up telling her my darkest secrets.

My best option is to remain silent. As awkward as it is.

I don't trust Lucy. Not yet. After she lost me in Paris today and acted like it was no big deal, I can't place my confidence in her. I just can't.

After we finish our meals, we fall into deeper silence. The waiter brings the check, and I'm relieved that it's time for us to leave. I put cash, tip included, in the envelope and signal to Lucy I was ready to leave.

At the hotel, Lucy asks if I want to join her for anther drink at the bar. "One and done?"

I wouldn't dare go through another round of painful interactions, so I tell Lucy I'm too tired and just want to crash in bed. We still have two days to explore the city. Sleep will do me good. Lucy thanks me for the dinner and announces she'd rather stay for one more. Of course she does. She's in her twenties, full of energy and vitality, in one of the most gorgeous places on Earth.

As I step in front of the elevator and wait for it to arrive, a man in his late forties stands next to me and gives me a suspicious look. I avoid his gaze, but I can feel his eyes boring into me. He looks like he wants to talk to me, but I'm in no mood to have a conversation with anybody. So, I take my phone out and pretend to be texting someone. I end up reading Skull's text for the hundredth time. *Lynn, we gotta meet up.*

I tried calling Skull several times, but the call didn't go through. Apparently, I couldn't dial anyone back home without the international plan, which I don't have. Fucking Europe. If I'd known this would be a problem, I would have chosen a more convenient destination. Like Puerto Rico.

But I could text him back when I was connected to Wi-Fi. I asked him repeatedly what he wanted to discuss, but he'd never responded.

Why would he torture me like this?

Why do we need to meet up? I'm starting to think that traveling to Paris wasn't the right move after all in terms of gaining clarity. My answer on the next steps is back home with Skull, who probably has a trick or two under his sleeve. Despite everything, he's always managed to evade death many times while dealing with his unsatisfied clients.

He must have found out that Jimmy has been reported missing. Has someone caught and reported him to the police? And did the police track him down right away? Is he in jail now, and is that why he hasn't responded to my numerous texts?

Oh, God, help me.

With every passing thought, my fear runs wild. The elevator arrives, and the gentleman standing next to me lets me in first. I'm still staring at my phone, and my shoulders sag with relief when the elevator dings. His room is on the top floor, as well. When we exit, he takes the right turn, and I take the left.

Our suite is made up, the bed sheets tucked in, the towels hanging nicely in the bathroom. Everything looks orderly, not like the way Lucy leaves it in a total mess when we're at home.

But I won't need to worry about it any longer.

I swiftly remove my luggage from the closet shelf and pack my clothes. They overflow, but I force myself to slow down and start putting them back in more carefully. I can't wait to get out of here. I look around the suite to make sure

I've got all my stuff, and before I exit the room, I take my phone out and text back Skull:

I'm in Paris, but I will be there soon. Let's meet.

I'm eager to escape the mounting tension and uncover the mystery Skull is about to reveal. I hasten my steps, walk through the door, and sneak my way through the lobby, hiding from Lucy who's still hanging at the bar. I make my way outside, unnoticed, take a left and walk an entire block.

Then I start looking for a cab to take me to the airport.

I STAY up having drinks at the bar way longer than expected.

It was partly down to meeting a lovely American couple at the bar. I'd ended up chatting with them until one in the morning. They'd recently got married and they were in Paris for their honeymoon. Every time I meet a happy couple, a sliver of jealousy rushes through me. They look so content, holding each other's hand, kissing, smiling at each other. It's obvious they're happy.

Will I ever get lucky to find someone who will adore me and take care of me? Sure, Evan does, but our feelings will never be mutual.

I say goodbye to the couple and go upstairs to my room, feeling sad. Other people's happiness gets to me sometimes, and I can't shake it off. I swing the door of our suite open and notice the eerie quietness. Only the occasional muffled honking on the streets project through the room's silence. The street our hotel is located is always busy with cars passing by at wee hour.

Lynn must be sound asleep in her room.

I go to bed and fall asleep immediately.

At nine in the morning, I peel my eyes open, greeted by another sunny day. We have a full itinerary around the city, and I should caffeinate myself enough to survive the day. I listen for sounds on the other side of my door, but I don't hear Lynn. I was hoping she'd already make coffee for us.

My phone on the nightstand lights up, so I reach for it, noticing a text message. I pick up my phone and bring it closer to my eyes. It's Evan. Speaking of the devil. I haven't contacted him once while in Paris, so I'm not surprised to hear from him.

Are you okay???

Three question marks. Is Evan panicking about my whereabouts? I imagine he can't shake the worry gnawing at him. I can picture him checking his phone repeatedly, hoping for a message or call that would ease his restless thoughts.

I put the phone back on the stand, ignoring Evan's text, and go to find Lynn. The coffee hasn't been made yet, and everything looks the same as last night.

Something is wrong.

I approach Lynn's door and knock, but I don't get an answer. I open the door slowly and call for her, anticipating an unwelcome scene.

The room is empty.

Though it looks as if she'd slept in her bed, the sheets and the cover have been straightened. I go to the bathroom, and her toiletry bag and toothbrush are missing. I exit the bathroom into her bedroom to look for her luggage, but it's not there.

Lynn is gone. Did she go home? Did she leave me here all alone?

A mix of confusion and hurt wash over me. Questions buzz in my mind like persistent bees. Why would she leave without telling me? I look around, thinking she might have left a note, but I see nothing. It's all very odd.

I walk outside and sit in a chair in the living area. That lying wretch is gone. I can devise my next steps in complete silence and peace.

HOME IS where I want to be, even though it's unsafe. I took the midnight flight, as luckily there was a spare seat available. The ticket was expensive but worth the cost.

As soon as the cab drops me off at the house from the airport, I hastily cross the front yard through the gate and storm inside. Darkness has enveloped the house, and the neighborhood is quiet. The ocean is turbulent, and it's windy outside, but there are no other sounds.

The house is eerily quiet. I drop my luggage on the floor and head for my bedroom. Inside the drawer, I find Jimmy's phone, its battery now depleted. I turn around and walk through the kitchen, then outside, heading for the cliff by the ocean at the outskirt of my house.

With difficulty, I get through the hedge separating my house and the steep cliff, and meander to the edge. Before I flick the phone into the ocean, I look around for traces of anyone watching me. At a far distance, I see a neighbor in his yard, sitting in his chair under the well-lit patio.

Shit.

Even though it's dark on my side, I can't risk exposing myself while throwing Jimmy's phone.

The man is sitting all alone and is reading with his head down. I will do it later. As soon as I wake up.

I go back to my house and grab my phone. When Lucy wakes up this morning, she'll see no traces of me. I'm sick to my stomach at the thought of what I've done. I've left her all alone in Paris. But she'll be fine. I know she will be.

Sorry, honey, but something urgent came up, and I had to come home. Be safe. I will see you tomorrow.

Tomorrow. She's coming home tomorrow.

I don't have much time to devise a plan.

Maybe I should go to bed right away and rest up, but unease is gnawing at me. The image of Lucy's smug face when I found her in the hotel lobby having a mimosa while I'd been roaming the streets of Paris, lost and panicked, still lingers in my mind. How could she be so blatantly careless about me?

I remember the little notebook she's hiding in the dresser drawer in her room. Maybe she's hiding key information inside. Could she be a spy or a CIA agent? Why hadn't I wondered about that before? After all, isn't she the one who stalked me endlessly when she discovered I was alive?

Not an ounce of me trusts Lucy.

I walk into her room, scared of what I might find. I wade through the clothes scattered on the floor and approach the dresser. A long sigh comes out of my mouth as I summon the inner strength to face whatever it is I'm about to discover. The notebook is still sitting in the same place I first found it. I unearth it, stare at it for a few long seconds, then open the first page.

A tattoo design. I flip to the next pages, but every page has a different tattoo design: dragons, flowers, ladybugs. Did Lucy draw all these? If she did, I was unaware of her artistic talents.

I've been deceived again. I put the notebook back in its place and go to bed, emotionally and mentally exhausted.

When I wake up in the morning, I'm struck with panic about how little time I have. My immediate plan is to call Skull and meet up with him, as per his request. I pick up the phone and dial his number.

"Hello?" His voice sounds rusty, as if he just awoke.

"Hi, Skull. It's Lynn. Where the hell have you been? I've been texting you forever."

"Sorry. I got a little busy. What's up?"

"I got your text that you want to meet up."

"Yes. We need to, Lynn." Now he sounds fully awake. "When is good?"

I shake my head, thinking, then the words come out of my mouth involuntarily. "Now."

"It would be best if we met at your place. Or mine. Whatever you prefer."

I look outside and think of my vast property. At the edge of the ocean, where other houses stick out at the periphery, anyone can see me, but my place is mostly hidden and offers a good level of privacy. But I'd rather do it at a different location where no soul can trace my steps.

"How about your place?" I ask.

"Yeah, sure. So, I don't get to see your mansion today?"

Neither of us laughs at his quip, which makes me realize we are in a grave and serious situation. I'm eager to hear what he has to say. Maybe he has thought of a plan to disguise Jimmy's death. It's in his interest, too, because he is the accessory to Jimmy's murder. We can't easily absolve him.

He is my partner in crime, whether he wants it or not.

I get ready and head over to Skull's place. When I arrive, he's sitting on the outside front steps, smoking a blunt. When he sees me, he flicks it in the air, and it lands close to my feet. His house is giant, which is not what I'd expected. I'd pictured Skull living in a small house, since he's been single all his life.

"Wow. So, this is where you're hiding?" I tell him, as I survey his vast property. It looks serene and isolate. There are no neighbors around, and the main street is nearly a mile away.

"Hiding?" He smirks.

"It's a joke."

Skull looks at me, his face serious.

He gets up and turns around to enter the house. I'd expected him to greet me with a hug, but as he comes closer, he just walks by, barely looking at me. I'm used to Skull's warmth, his affection and caring he has shown me over the past years. What has happened to him?

The more I observe him, the more I notice how different his disposition is. His tense body looks to be boiling with rage.

"Should we go inside?"

"Sure."

He lets me walk by him, and he follows me. As we enter, I'm struck by the interior of his house. It looks more sophisticated than the outside, and I'd never imagined it being this way. His house is a cozy haven, with warm colors and comfortable furnishings that invite a sense of home. The living room boasts a plush sofa and a well-loved coffee table adorned with scattered books and family photos. There are photos of him when he was younger, and I barely recognize him with a full set of hair on his head. A photo of a young boy sits beside him, and I'm itching to ask about his identity, but the timing isn't ideal. I'm here with one mission in mind.

"Would you like something to drink?"

"No. No, thanks."

He's walking around the living room, his eyes darting around as if he's looking for something. If he's angered by something I've done, he doesn't say anything. This is a Skull I'm not used to: he can be opinionated, but his silence signals something else, and it irritates me no end. There's a shift in our dynamics for reasons unbeknownst to me.

"Can I sit down? You wanted to talk," I chime in. As I point at the couch, I notice my hand trembling. What's Skull about to say?

I sit down, and he follows suit. We sit across from one another, facing each other squarely.

"Word got around that you've found your daughter," he says.

I smile. "Yes. Can you believe it? In a million years, I never would have thought this could happen."

He shrugs. "All kinds of things happen in life."

"I guess." I put my head down, grab the seam of my dress, and twirl it around my finger.

"Where is she now?"

"Right now? She's in Paris. On vacation." I nod quickly and feel the heat shoot up to my cheeks. If he only knew I left her all alone in a big city without giving her advance notice. What kind of mother would he think I am?

A shitty one.

"Paris?" His eyes bulge at me. "When is she coming back?"

"Tomorrow." My head is still bobbing. But why all the questions about Lucy? I'm assuming he's not here to learn about my daughter, however curious he might be about the miracle of discovering she's alive. "Why am I here, Skull? What did you want to talk to me about?" I find my strength to get to the point. A clock chimes from the mantlepiece and I glance in its direction. Propped up against it is an official-looking envelope addressed to Skull, though of course they've used his real name.

Evan.

Is Evan his real name?

Skull clears his throat. "Have you heard Jimmy has been reported missing?"

"I did. Yes."

He moves forward and places his elbows on his lap, as his gigantic eyes bore into me. "What are we going to do about it?"

I RETURN HOME from Paris with a mission on my mind.

It's two o'clock in the afternoon, and the house is empty. I drop all my bags by the front door and proceed inside the house. I strain to hear any sounds, but it's awfully quiet here. Lynn must be in her room or by the pool, resting.

I'm still processing the fact that Lynn left me behind in Paris with no notice. She texted me to apologize but said nothing about what prompted the sudden departure. What could be so important to make her up and leave in the middle of the night without letting me know? Her sudden departure from Paris only raised my suspicions. My probing questions about Jimmy at our last dinner must have triggered something that caused her to flee.

For the same reason, I don't trust Lynn at all anymore.

She's been hiding something from me, and I need to know what it is.

"Mom!" I call for Lynn, but I get no answer. "Mom! Are you home?"

I'm grateful she's not here. I go to my room and then freeze as I enter. All the drawers of my dresser are wide open, and some of my clothes from the dresser are down on the floor. Lynn must have done this, but why? What was she hoping to find?

I exit my room and go down the stairs to look for Lynn by the pool, but she's not there. Where could she be? She didn't leave any signs of her whereabouts in the house. Maybe she went out for lunch with a friend or a walk by the beach? The past month we've lived together, Lynn has rarely left the house. She prefers to spend time in the confines of her bedroom walls. She said once she was still savoring the new home and liked to be on her own. It seems odd she prefers solitude, but I haven't questioned her.

When I walk past the kitchen table, an object catches my eye. A phone. Lynn must have forgotten it. I pick it up and turn it on. The light beams up to my face. My stomach lurches.

This isn't Lynn's phone.

As I study the screen, the room starts to spin. This phone belongs to Jimmy.

My heart quickens. A surge of uncertainty washes over me, and curiosity and apprehension battle inside my mind. The device sits innocently on the table, its screen reflecting an unseen list of messages and calls, mostly mine. I snatch it up, almost on instinct, my mind racing with questions. What secrets might this device hold? Will it unravel the enigma of Jimmy's disappearance?

But most importantly: what is Jimmy's phone doing in our house?

I STORM out of the house with Jimmy's phone. I'm starving, but food can wait.

I get into my car and head out to the familiar place I always head to when I need to clear my head. Traffic is light, so it should take no time to get there. As I drive, I check out my surroundings, hoping to find Lynn and shake the shit out of her, but there's only a few passersby walking on the curbs.

Lynn owes me an explanation. Like how did she get ahold of Jimmy's phone and what was she doing with it? Or why was she lying during dinner in Paris? Things are not adding up, and something sinister is at play, I'm getting surer of it by the minute.

By the beach, I park my car and stroll past the well-known ice cream shop, observing a line of people patiently waiting outside. All these years I've come to this neighborhood, I haven't set foot in that ice cream shop once, but at that moment, I resolve to visit after all the dust settles. Because I love ice cream. Chocolate is my favorite.

A few blocks from the beach, I arrive at my familiar place, the row of tiny houses that seem to never change. Except for Lynn's old house.

Several construction workers are roaming around, carrying building materials and leaving them in the front yard. The house is wide open; the windows stripped naked. There's a guy on the roof, walking around and inspecting it. The landlord has clearly done renovations in the house now that nobody lives there.

I turn off the engine, exit the car, and walk to the house to search for clues about Jimmy's disappearance. One of the construction workers turns in my direction and says, "Can I help you?"

"Hi. Yes. I'm the daughter of the couple who used to live here. Do you mind if I go inside and walk around? My mom lost her ring and was hoping I would find it here."

He shrugs and makes a face, pointing at the house. "Be my guest."

"Thank you."

I walk inside the house, finding zero traces of Jimmy's and Lynn's life inside.

The floor is completely naked, revealing the white cement. The faded, brown walls have lost their vibrancy, and the ceilings look as if they're about to collapse. And the stench—even though the house is devoid of any physical evidence of my parents having lived here—is unbearable. It seems like the smell of alcohol has saturated these walls, and it will take a few layers of paint to get rid of it.

How on earth were they able to live here? How did they sustain their marriage for all these years and survived it? I observed it only from a distance, but now that I'm walking through the house and trying to relive their past, I'm astounded and saddened by their fate.

I walk through the house, my eyes peeled on the floor, but no physical items remain anywhere. This place won't give me any clues about what might have happened to Jimmy or where he is now.

A construction worker comes inside and walks by me, giving me a strange look. He says nothing and minds his own business. This house needs a major overhaul, and while I'm sad it will erase my parents' entire past, I'm glad that a lucky person will get to claim it. The location is prime at least.

Disappointed to walk back empty-handed, I head for the car. Then I hear my name being called from nearby. I turn in the voice's direction and notice a tiny woman standing by the fence next door.

I squint to take a better look and immediately recognize her. It's Rose. When I first met her at our housewarming party, I'd found her annoying and nosy, but today, the sight of her makes me smile. She'd be a perfect person to ask questions. Maybe she knows something I don't.

"Hi, Rose." I wave at her as I head closer.

"Oh, hi, dear. So good to see you again." Her face glimmers with joy. "I've been thinking about you lately.

How are things?" She leans forward and whispers as she winks at me. "And how's the new mom?"

I laugh. "Mom is good." I shrug. "Yeah, nothing new to report. Still getting to know each other."

She nods. "That's good. That's good."

I crane my neck to look over her shoulder and notice a small pile of scraps. Looks like trash she's hoarded over the years. It's amazing what mind and body can do when living alone.

She follows my gaze and turns around to stare at the pile. "You're looking at that?"

"I didn't mean to, sorry. It just drew my attention."

"No worries, dear." She leans forward. "Do you want to know what it is?"

I hate to admit it, but I'm curious. "Sure."

"It's the stuff I found in their house." She points toward Lynn's old house. "The landlord came by the other day and told me he couldn't get a hold of either Lynn or Jimmy, so he asked me if I could collect the little of their stuff left behind. I figured maybe Lynn would want it at some point, so I went inside and grabbed it all."

"That's nice of you, Rose."

She smiles. "I try. I really try. They were good neighbors."

Her lips twitch and I can tell she's dying to tell me something that's been lingering on her mind.

"What is it?" I ask.

"Among the stuff I found, there was a letter."

"A letter?"

"Yeah." She nods. She places her index finger across her lips and bulges her eyes to mimic shock. "Do you know who the letter is from?"

"Who?"

"It's from a lawyer." She comes closer and whispers. "Jimmy has another daughter. Her name is Emma."

Nothing new there. I nod and tell her I already knew. Lowering her gaze, she seemed hurt that she couldn't be the bearer of this shocking news.

"Rose, can you tell me if you've seen Jimmy recently at all? I mean, has he come to the house by any chance?"

Rose's smile dissipates, and the sparkle in her eyes disappears. "Haven't you heard?"

Fear shoots up my spine. "Heard what?"

"Jimmy has been reported missing. No one knows where he's gone to."

"YOU'RE ASKING *me* what to do about it?" I nearly scream at Skull after he poses the question.

The weather outside is beckoning. My preference is to spend my time walking on the beach, not plotting with Skull to outsmart the police. We'd better find an exit from this terrifying ordeal.

Skull is pacing around his living room, back and forth, back and forth, appearing to be thinking. He stops in the middle and looks at me. "Who do you think reported him missing?"

I scoff. "How the fuck would I know, Skull?" I monitor his actions to evaluate his response. But Skull looks way too nervous for me to believe he has orchestrated this whole thing. We are on the same team, trying to figure this out together.

Get away with murder.

"Just because he's missing doesn't mean they might think he's dead." He gives a quick nod and says, "Right?"

I shrug my shoulders, unsure of what to say. "I don't know how long cops look for a person of interest before they declare them dead. Jesus, haven't you been in a similar situation in the past? I mean with your line of work?"

Skull has gotten away from a lot of trouble in the past. I deem him an expert. But I don't get the answer I desperately seek. He gives me a menacing look instead—he doesn't seem to appreciate my question. "What the fuck, Lynn? My line of work? I work in construction, for crying out loud!"

"Construction?" all these years, I've believed that dealing drugs is Skull's main calling. It just tells you how little I know about him. "I had no idea you were in construction."

Skull looks at me and shakes his head. "It's no one's business what I do on the side."

"I'm sorry. I thought you might know what happens when a person is gone missing. I mean, I hate to state the obvious, but Jimmy is dead. Lying on the bottom of the ocean." I pause before I prepare myself with the burning question. "Have you told anyone?"

Skull stops in the middle of the room and gives me a deadly look. I've never seen him so rattled. A sliver of fear runs through me, as Skull clenches and unclenches his fists and raises one up in the air.

"Stop it!" Skull yells. His brows are stitched together in anger. He marches around his living room again, whispering words under his breath. I can't hear him, but I would love to know what he's thinking. Time is of the essence. We need to come up with a plan quickly.

We both resort to silence when a sudden thought occurs to me. Shit, I left Jimmy's phone behind, on the kitchen table after failing to dash it in the ocean. Shit! It's too late to go back home and hide it. Lucy should be home any minute. She texted me from the airport when she landed as I drove to Skull's place.

I get up from the couch, anxiety shooting down my spine. Skull notices my panicky demeanor. "What's wrong?"

"I just remembered I left Jimmy's phone on the kitchen table. When Lucy comes home, she'll find it, no doubt."

Skull momentarily halts and thrusts his arms in the air. "And? Your point?"

"Don't you see? She'll find his phone and wonder what it's doing there. Fuck! We're fucked, Skull. Lucy is smart. She'll probably find his phone, wonder what it's doing there, and figure out I killed him."

Skull's eyes bulge.

"She called him so many times after I gave her his number. When she realized he'd never call back, she got disappointed. Like, *really* disappointed."

Skull watches me with curious eyes but doesn't say anything. He wants me to keep speculating what might happen when—not if—Lucy locates Jimmy's phone.

"Listen, Skull. I'm afraid that Lucy has suspected something all along. See what I'm saying?"

He shakes his head, as if not understanding the implication of this. "No, Lynn. Tell me. What are you saying?"

I put my head down in shame, but the thoughts running through my head are the only ones that make sense right now. Call me desperate, but I can think of only one solution to this terrible problem. "Lucy is trouble. And I don't trust her. She has suspected something is wrong all along."

I turn around and do my meditation move, where I deeply inhale and then exhale with my eyes closed. Skull is rooted to his spot, awaiting the punch line. Now that I've gathered my thoughts, I turn around to face Skull again and deliver the plan that will be advantageous to both of us.

I sigh. "We should get rid of Lucy."

Skull walks away, mumbling under his breath. What is he saying? I really want to hear him. If he agrees, we'd better think of a plan quickly. Make it look like an accident. Like Jimmy had done to me. But Skull doesn't look keen. He punches the wall and yells out from the top of his lungs, "What?! What the fuck is wrong with you, you damn fucking whore?"

I WANT TO THROW UP. Jimmy's missing? So, everyone seems to know. The word has clearly gone around.

I stare at Rose, barely finding words and then struggling to get them out of my mouth. "How long?"

"No one really knows. Somebody reported him missing about a week ago."

A week ago. That's around the same time the cop came to visit our house. He must have visited to ask Lynn about Jimmy's whereabouts. Lynn had looked nervous as I watched them through the window. I also recall Lynn telling me the cop came to ask about her health conditions.

Another lie.

"What was the last time you saw Jimmy? Had he visited the house at all since they left?" I look in the house's direction. The construction workers are minding their own business and have no clue about the dire conversation I'm having with the neighbor.

She looks up at the sky to think, then shuts her eyes

tightly. She looks at me. "Oh, it's been quite a while. Even before they moved to the new place."

They?

"Rose, I have to ask." I pause for a second to find a delicate balance in my question delivery. "Is it you who reported him missing?"

Her head snaps back and she makes a face. "Me? Are you crazy?"

"Who could it be?"

She shrugs, looking bewildered. "Beats me."

I'm acting surprised that Rose didn't report Jimmy missing. But, to be fair, I shouldn't be.

Because it was me who called the cops.

After so many attempts to reach Jimmy, I gave in and suspected something might have happened to him. Maybe he's been abducted by a crazy person, or perhaps he's lying lifeless in a ditch somewhere.

No one ignores anybody for this long. I just want someone to find him, so I can shake the shit out him and ask him why he has been ignoring me.

But now, I suspect that Lynn has something to do with it. His phone at our house, the cop visiting. What else? Lies piled up on top of lies. My head is spinning, and I'm shaking from disbelief.

Did Lynn murder Jimmy? Could she have?

Before I find Lynn and confront her, I have one more place to visit.

"I have to go, Rose. Thanks for the all the info." Before I turn around and leave, my eyes rest on the pile of trash, and I tell myself I'll have to come back to go through it.

"Where are you going, dear?"

Saying nothing, I wave at her goodbye and storm into my car, before turning the engine on and pushing hard on the accelerator. I'm driving, but I barely paying attention to the roads, stuck in the cycle of shock and disbelief.

Fifteen minutes later, I arrive at the town hall. Parking is easy during this time of day on a Monday. There's barely anyone around. I hasten my steps and look for the record section. The hallway is empty. The grandeur and vastness of the building's ceiling cause my footsteps to echo. I finally see the sign labeled as PUBLIC RECORDS and notice a computer beneath it.

Lynn recently told me she and Jimmy were getting divorced. And that it's been in the process for a while. Her lawyer is finalizing all the paperwork. But it's been filed, and they're just waiting for the date of their hearing.

I sit in the chair at the computer and locate the password taped on top of the screen. As my hands hover over the overused keyboard, they shake. And I don't think it's my hunger that's causing it. Was Lynn telling me yet another lie? If records don't show up, it will be as clear as day.

The computer's screen lights up when I put in the password. Several icons appear, and my eyes hastily dart around to find the right one.

DIVORCE RECORDS

I hover the mouse over it and click on it. The next

thing that jumps out is a box that says ENTER NAME, so I click on that next and slowly type my mother's name: LYNN MILLER.

Five entries come up, all with a middle name included. I'm embarrassed to say, but I do not know my mother's middle name. Or if she has one. I only know her age. She was born on February 25, 1965, in New Hampshire. But if there are any records of her divorce filing, Jimmy's name should be listed.

I click on the first record and notice it's from decades ago. A Lynn Miller divorcing her husband, Steven Miller, because of irreconcilable differences. Anxious, I go to the next record, revealing an entirely different couple. When I get to the last record, I hope it's the one.

It isn't.

I feel sick to my stomach. I can't go home and face Lynn just yet. After I get in my car, I head into the familiar direction. Evan's house. He is the only who will understand what is going on in my life.

"WHAT ARE YOU SAYING, SKULL?" My voice comes out high pitched and panicked. He stands up and walks up to the picture of his son, lifts it up, and stares at it. "Talk to me for fuck's sake. Tell me why you're doing this."

I can't help but scream. Skull is acting so calm, as if he didn't just tell me he was going to go to the cops to confess everything. He's going to tell them the sequence of events and how he aided Jimmy's body disposal.

"I'm sorry, Lynn. I've already decided."

He puts the photo down and walks back to the couch.

"This makes no sense! Of all people, I trusted you the most. I paid you to keep your mouth shut, didn't I? A hundred k. That's a lot of money, Skull. Do you want more? Is this what's all about?"

He shakes his head and looks off into the distance. "No. It's not about money, Lynn." He's so calm I want to punch him in the face.

"Then what is it? It's not like you've ever done

anything similar before. Why now? What is going on? Tell me."

"You're a danger to society, Lynn. You've acted like a lunatic, and I'm afraid you're going to harm more people."

"What? What the fuck are you saying? Who the fuck are you to tell me all this? Since when are you judging me?"

I'm so mad I'm about to burst at the seams. There's something Skull isn't telling me, and he's blaming me instead.

I shake my head in disbelief and throw my arms overhead. My face flushes with anger, and I walk in small circles, contemplating my next steps. Shit. If Skull confesses, I'm fucked. I'm done. I will go to jail and spend the rest of my life there.

My brain is spinning, thinking of the next steps, but I'm so rattled that nothing comes to mind.

Skull gets up from the couch and approaches me, putting his hands on my back. "Now, leave."

I can't believe he's kicking me out. "What?"

He pushes me with such a force that I almost fall to the ground, but I somehow find a balance. "Skull, no, no. Please." I don't want to leave his house. I can still convince him to be on my side. I can offer him a lot more money than he would ever expect. "How about a million dollars? Please. Take it. No one needs to find out what we've done. Please."

Skull doesn't care what I have to say. My pleas land on his deaf ears. He keeps pushing me, and tears fall from my eyes as he opens the front door and gives me the last shove. I wipe my eyes as I enter my car, feeling lost. I don't know what I should do next, nor where I should go.

Distressed, I head toward my home, hoping and praying that Skull will change his mind in the meantime. It's possible he will, because I can't think of one reason he would benefit from it.

But if he doesn't, I have only one way out.

JUST AS I pull into Evan's driveway, I see a car parked in the front. It's a Toyota, the same color as Lynn's. Weird coincidence. I'm hesitant to get closer. If Evan has a guest, I don't want to intrude. I put the car in reverse and park behind a tree, curious about who his guest might be. While hidden behind the tree, I take a better look at Evan's property.

Evan's backyard is a peaceful retreat, blending natural beauty with thoughtful landscaping. A well-manicured lawn sprawls beneath the shade of mature trees, providing a cool haven on warm days. A wooden deck adorned with comfortable seating extends from the house, offering a perfect spot for outdoor gatherings and relaxation. Surrounding the yard are blossoming flower beds and potted plants, adding bursts of color and a touch of nature's grace. When does he take time to take care of it all? This is the tender Evan I rarely get to see, because I refuse to give him a chance.

While waiting for the guest to leave, I pull my phone out and text Rebecca. Her communication has been sporadic since the housewarming party. I'm hoping she'll come around, and our friendship will resume. Since reuniting with Lynn, I've never felt lonelier.

The three dots appear, signaling Rebecca's typing, and then they halt. There's no message coming my way.

I look up and see the front door opening, and I do a double take when I see the familiar face coming out of Evan's house.

My chest constricts and my legs almost give way beneath me.

What on earth is Lynn doing at Evan's house? And how does she know him?

I lean forward to take a better look and then see her distressed face. She looks like she's crying. I shake my head in confusion, whispering to myself, "What the fuck is going on here?"

Lynn enters her Toyota, turns the engine on, and pulls out of the driveway, heading in the opposite direction. She didn't see me. Perhaps I should follow her, but I'm too stunned to move.

I sit back, leaning against my seat, gasping in confusion. Evan has a lot of explaining to do. My car engine is still on, so I push the accelerator pedal and move toward the driveway. I park in the front, where Lynn's car sat just a minute ago, and exit my car, shuffling to the front door.

Evan is sitting on the couch with his head down. He

looks like someone has been beating him senseless for hours. His cell phone is clutched tightly in his hand.

I say nothing at first and look around to check for any evidence of Lynn's presence. I notice one of his son's photos has been moved from its old place, just a few inches to the right. He hadn't touched that photo in a while, and I wonder what prompted moving it today.

"Evan?"

He doesn't even flinch at my voice. "Evan, please talk to me. I need to know what my mother was doing at your place."

My voice is etched with impatience. Evan looks up, and a tear moves down his cheek. I'd never expect such a display of sadness from a man exuding masculinity. "Oh, my God, Evan."

I approach and sit next to him, holding his hand. "Please tell me what's going on." I put my hand on his and lightly squeeze it.

He looks at me with damp eyes. "I'm a bad person, Lucy." He wipes his cheeks with one hand, puts his head down, and continues, "But I love you."

Police sirens echo in a distance until they get closer. They stop in front of the house, and the sirens go dead. What are they doing here? I want to ask Evan, but I'm out of time. He covers his face with his hands, then sobs.

I CAN'T BELIEVE this fucker is ratting me out.

Sure, there's a chance he won't, but my gut tells me he's set his mind and won't change it. All these years, I could trust Skull with my life, but trust can be fleeting, even with the closest to us. Now that I'm reflecting on my relationship with him, he was nothing more than my drug dealer. I know nothing about his past, or his family affairs, where he came from, what his dreams and aspirations are.

The more I think about it, the more I realize I didn't even know his real name until I saw that envelope on his mantlepiece.

Skull. It's a stupid damn nickname.

I'm driving around like a crazy person. I wish I had a place to hide, but heaven knows I've burned so many bridges in life. Even if I find a place to hide, the cops will find me. The vast world contracts when justice calls.

But if my plan works out, I might escape from the clutches of the police force.

I pull into my driveway and close the gate. The lock is stuck, and it won't budge, so I yank it harder until it's put in place. As I'm about to secure the lock, I hear the police sirens getting closer to my house, and I know they're here for me.

In my peripheral vision, I notice James, the retired cop, patrolling around the street. Maybe he has nothing better to do with his time? Or perhaps he knew more than I thought and wanted to investigate more deeply.

But I don't have time to talk to him or confront him. Because Skull has confessed.

As the sound of sirens echo closer, my eyes roll back in my sockets, and I feel I'm about to faint. The survival mode kicks in, and I run across the yard to reach the back of my house. Behind me, I hear a car screeching to a halt, then a cop screaming for me to stop. But I don't. I run across the front yard, fueled by adrenaline and fear. I can't picture myself rotting in prison now that a better life has been dangled in front of me.

The gate rattles with an incredible noise that gets muffled as soon as I make a turn around the house. Several cops are yelling, each instructing where to go. I look over my shoulder and see Danny running in my direction. I jump over the hedge separating the house and the ocean. The deep water beckons me, and I tell myself it's time.

The cliff is about ten feet tall from the water surface, and I tell myself a jump will be manageable. I leap from the cliff into the depth of the ocean. The impact of smashing into the water wakes all my senses. The summer is at the end of its tail, but the water remains as cold as ice. I can still swim. My swimming skills from when I was younger and vigorous come in handy now, but the ocean is uncooperative today, and I'm having a difficult time swimming fast.

I look up and see a head peeking from above. A cop has spotted me and is watching me struggle. I'm convinced my escape is futile now, but I keep swimming with only hope left to propel me ahead. A splash near me makes me turn around, and I see Danny's head poke up from the ocean. He's behind me, swimming in my direction. I stop, because I'm too weak to make any significant progress. The next thing I feel is Danny grabbing me under the arm and saying, "I got you."

My head is barely above the water, and I struggle to breathe or to move. Danny is doing his best to drag me sideways across the ocean to the coastline. It feels like miles. At the shallow part of the shore, a few cops are lined up and waiting for us. They watch Danny make small progress as he struggles to keep me above the water. At that very moment, I don't mind being swallowed by the ocean. I'll happily share Jimmy's fate. Because what awaits me on the ground, I imagine, is a long and thorny life.

One cop grabs me by the arms and pulls me out of the water. He is too rough and doesn't seem to care. His hard grip is hurting me. Then I'm lying on the ground, looking up at the sky and I wonder if this might be the last time I enjoy its vastness.

WHEN THE COPS arrive at Evan's house, they walk calmly inside as if they've just visited for a cup of coffee. They don't use force or display bouts of aggression. One of them looks at Evan and says, "Are you Evan Blake?"

He hovers over him, and Evan nods in agreement. "I am."

"You called the cops earlier. Correct?"

Evan nods again and puts his head down in shame. He gets up from the couch and extends his arms toward the cop. The cop pulls the handcuffs from his belt and places them around Evan's wrists. Evan glances at me and gives me a quick smile, but I imagine he's dealing with a whirlwind of emotions.

"Why are you taking him?" I ask, but the cop gives me a funny look and ignores me.

I don't understand any of this. Why did Lynn come visit Evan, and what's their connection? What has Evan done, and why are they taking him away?

All the secrets Lynn hid from me will surface soon, and I'll finally get the clarity I've been searching for.

But why Evan? What has he done to warrant an arrest?

The cops take him under his arm and walk him to their car. They shove him in the back and drive away. I'm left standing in the cloud of dust and I wave, feeling stupid for it. Evan doesn't turn around to face me. His head is down, and all I can see is the car becoming a smudge in the distance.

I hop in my car, finding no reason to stay around. Lynn is key to all the information, so I must find her next. On my way home, I'm hit with an unexplainable sense of doom. The walls are crashing on me.

Another surprise awaits me when I get home.

Several cop cars are parked in the front, and a small group of locals gather around, watching the scene unfolding. They're taking pictures, playing on their phone, maybe texting their loved ones to inform them of the crime scene related to their new neighbor. As I stand on the edge of the curb, I watch two cops leading Lynn toward their car. Lynn is soaking, water dripping from her hair and the dress. She looks small, standing between the two large cops.

I recognize the cop who came to visit the other day, and he's holding Lynn's arm. He's wet, too, his face serious and focused. Lynn doesn't strain against the force they're putting on her. Whatever resolve she has is now on a full display. She has given in.

Our eyes meet. But not for long. Lynn puts her head down immediately, avoiding me. Guilt and shame ooze out of her. A tear prickles out of my eye.

I want to ask the cop what's happening, but words elude me. I clutch Jimmy's phone, and it occurs to me then that the missing Jimmy must be dead somewhere, murdered by his wife. Or Evan? I still don't know how they got to be partners in the crime. Were they lovers? Did Lynn cheat on Jimmy with Evan, and Jimmy got killed in a jealous fight?

I've heard stories like this often. But all I feel is betrayal, as the people closest to me are taken away to jail. The cops open the back door of the car and push Lynn inside. She remains unfazed. She doesn't turn around to look at me.

It's as if I don't exist.

The car drives away, the sirens muted, and the group of the locals dissolves. I shuffle through the front yard, watching the ocean's waves serve as a turbulent backdrop to my mood. What's next? I go inside the house and look for something to eat in the fridge. I stare blankly at whatever is inside, losing my appetite at the thought of what I'd just witnessed. The house feels cold even though it is seventy-five degrees outside, and the sun beckons high in the sky. I stand in the kitchen and spin around, feeling lost.

But a sense of relief gets the better of me. Finally, they caught Lynn and I'm happy about it.

Two Months Later

I'M IN A SMALL, chilly place with bars all around. Just recently, I'd watched Dateline shows in the comfort of my home, about incarcerated murderers. I never thought this would be my life.

The lights above are bright, making the gray walls seem even more lifeless. This is far from the big house I'd recently lived in. Now I'm trapped in a small space that matches the confinement in my mind.

It makes me sick to my stomach when I think about this, but apparently, they found and excavated Jimmy's body from the depth of the ocean. Since the duffle bags were secured shut, his dismembered body parts were still somewhat intact. Shortly after, they scheduled his burial and now the pieces of him are resting in the Hampton town cemetery.

I've been here for almost a month, awaiting a court hearing to deliberate my sentence. No one has visited me yet. Lucy, my own daughter, now feels like a dream, a distant memory I never quite got to fully process. The uncertainty is thick, and I can't see what comes after this bleak place.

Time goes slowly here. Each hour feels like it's taking forever, and the air is heavy. The women I've met here all have a story to tell about why they're here: drug trafficking, murdering their own children, assaulting a police officer, you name-it. The most common one seems to be murder stemming from domestic abuse, but even in self-defense, no one is absolved from taking another human's life.

My thoughts keep going back to what happened, the choices I made, and the secrets I kept. It all echoes in the surrounding emptiness.

Sometimes, the guards come by with keys jingling, and the doors creak open. Their serious faces remind me I'm in a serious situation. The routine in the cell is repetitive, each moment getting me closer to facing the consequences in court. Am I bound to do this for the rest of my life?

Alone in my cell, I think about the daughter I thought I lost and the daughter I still have. Now I feel guilty for weaving a web of lies that she's caught in.

I hear footsteps and quiet talks from other people in nearby cells. The guard approaches my cell and announces, "You've got a visitor."

My immediate thought goes to my daughter, like it does every time he announces that someone is here to see me. I don't ask who it is. I don't want disappointment to reach me sooner if it's someone other than Lucy.

He unlocks the barred door and walks me to the visitor section. I'm shivering from anticipation, but as soon as I reach the visiting area, the sight of my attorney sitting on the other side of the visiting booth deflates my hope. Lucy will never visit me, I'm almost sure of it.

The court had appointed an attorney, but I'm rich enough to hire my own. If I'm to get away with a shorter sentence, I need a talented attorney by my side. Someone to get the jury to sympathize with my case. Because, fuck, how is this possibly all my fault?

I sit down at the booth and grab the phone hanging on the wall. My attorney, Nick, is all dressed up in what appears to be a new suit, and a new haircut. His smile is conspicuous, as if it could be a prelude to a piece of good news. When I heard he'd barely lost a case, I paid him a hefty bill just to secure his representation. After the final court hearing, I'll owe him a lot more. The lottery money is going away as fast as it came.

I grab the phone, but I say nothing. Not hello, nothing.

"Hey, Lynn."

I nod instead and wait to hear what he has to say.

His eyes droop down, then lift with renewed energy. "Your court hearing is scheduled for tomorrow. We should plead guilty for a third-degree murder."

My heart sinks when he delivers the words.

"Not a manslaughter?" I say.

He shakes his head. "The jury will have a hard time believing the murder wasn't premeditated. Especially since it wasn't in self-defense of any kind. Your husband was sleeping when you struck him with the cast iron pan. They will not see it as anything but a murder."

"What about all the things he'd done prior? He tampered with my brakes, driving me to death. How's that not enough proof?"

Nick is quiet for what seems to be forever, looking me straight in the eye. "There's no way to prove that he had something to do with the brakes. But if the jury finds he was after you, that's the only thing that will separate you from a first and a third-degree murder. But there's only circumstantial evidence."

"I know he was after me. I can't prove it, but I believe it."

Another pause that gives me bad vibes. "Belief isn't treated as proof in court. But it could help a little. If you get trialed with a third-degree murder, we're looking at the sentence of forty years. We have a strong case that you were under duress. Emotionally unstable. The pressure that your husband was putting on you to buy a house ... and the physical abuse. I think we have something here." He smiles.

All the beatings and coercions over the years seem like they could come in handy now, for the sake of reclaiming my freedom. But really—no one knows the suffering I've experienced under the roof of that tiny row house.

I nod. "Okay."

"Get some rest for tomorrow. The hearing starts bright and early. Eight a.m. The guards will give you a ride to the court. I'll see you then."

He hangs up the phone and gets up. It's time to put the lottery money to work. Will it save me from a lifetime imprisonment?

IF THERE'S anything I could ever depend on in life, it's my instincts.

Deep down I think a part of me knew Jimmy was dead when he didn't rely to my emails.

I'm sick to my stomach that Lynn killed him. The day Evan confessed, the cops took both into a police station and jailed them without bail.

Evan's story was a lot simpler than Lynn's.

At the courtroom, Evan had gazed in my direction occasionally, his eyes drooping in sadness. Handcuffs hugged his wrists, but it didn't strike me that Evan would try to escape. He was there to confess his crimes and serve a sentence.

His sentence? Two and a half years in prison and a fine of one thousand dollars. If he didn't confess himself, it would have been a lot harsher.

His defense attorney had leaned toward him and whispered something in his ear. Evan nodded and put his head down, as if feeling shame. The guards approached him and ordered him to stand up. Evan turned around to look at me one more time, and as he extended his arms to be taken away to prison, he gave me a smile. Did he do all this for me? Did he think I was in danger being surrounded by the monster we know Lynn is?

When I came out of the courtroom, I saw a familiar face standing in the hallway. As soon as she spoke, I recognized the voice. Lynn's friend, Barbara.

"Don't you remember me?" she said.

"Now I do." What was she doing at Evan's hearing?

She smiled. "I'm here for Skull."

"Skull?"

"Our friend, Skull. Evan. Everyone knows him by his nickname."

Except me, apparently.

"How do you know him?"

"Oh, we go way back." She waves her arm. "We're good friends."

I stare at her, piecing together the friendship triangle between Evan—or should I say, Skull—Barbara, and Lynn. The only ties I saw that connected them were drugs.

"He's been telling me about you," she continues. "You know, he never really talks about a woman, but he somehow found something special in you. His life has been so tragic that he doesn't get close to anyone. For whatever reason, he seemed taken by you. He showed me your picture one day and bragged about you. It didn't occur to me at the party that that's where I'd seen you before."

I didn't know if I should be happy or terrified to hear this.

But now I've learned about all of their abhorrent pasts, I plan to move on with my life. I plan on selling the house. I'm going to move to North Carolina. There's nothing in New Hampshire to keep me around. I want to live near my father, the one who has been there for me through the worst.

It's not the parents we choose, but the parents who choose us. Choose to love us. Be with us. Never give up on us.

It has become painfully apparent that Lynn's and Jimmy's marriage was a failure. Arguments, like storms, would erupt unpredictably, thundering through their home. Violence, a twisted form of communication in their flawed dynamic, became the default solution to their problems. Witnessing their inability to navigate conflicts without resorting to physicality was a sobering recognition, a reminder that their home was a battleground rather than a sanctuary.

It pains me to know that my biological parents were two pieces of shit.

I pay Evan a visit in jail one more time before I disappear from his life. It's raining, dampening the already sour mood, but I do my best to ignore it. My whole life is ahead of me, and I will work harder on making it a good one. Maybe I'll go back to school and finish it, build a career, find a good therapist to talk out the issues of my fear of abonnement. I'm young, and there are so many opportunities ahead of me.

The guard leads me to a room with a row of small booths separated by glass partitions, and telephones hang on the wall on each side. My first time visiting a penitentiary. And my last. A guard on the other side leads Evan all the way to the booth and instructs him to sit down across from me.

Evan's face brightens when he sees me, and a big smile forms on his face. He picks up the phone from the wall and says nothing at first. As silence carries between us, I see shame and sadness. Even in this short timeframe, he's lost some weight. His hollowed cheeks emphasize his underlying bone structure, giving a true meaning to his nickname.

"Hi." He breaks the silence.

 "Hello."

"Thanks for visiting me," he says, his gaze fixed on me, as if he longs to touch me. "I've missed you."

I nod and say nothing. He seems to notice that I'm not reciprocating, so the smile on his face disappears.

He continues, "I haven't really had anyone visit me. I just miss having a normal conversation."

"I get it." I say it like I'm empathizing. "I do. Two and a half years isn't so bad."

He gazes downward and nods. I guess it's easier for me to say than it is for somebody who won't taste freedom for a long time. All the things he will miss out on. Another chance to reconcile and repair his relationship with his son. A chance to enjoy the nature and freedom. To go sit at a restaurant and have a delicious meal. All the things we sometimes take for granted. Honestly, I don't envy him.

"I suppose," he says, "I don't regret confessing."

I tilt my head and narrow my eyes at that. "Yeah, why did you confess? I'm dying to know."

His eyes bulge at me, and for a second, he looks over his shoulder to ensure no one is listening, but I bet they wired all the phones, and that all conversations are monitored. Nothing remains a secret between these gray, lonely walls.

"When you didn't respond for that week when you were in Paris, I had this idea that Lynn might have hurt you. I freaked out. Lynn is a crazy bitch, you know. Something has happened to her since she won the lottery. She's not the same woman I met thirty years ago. I know she's your mother, but—"

I interrupt him and wave my free hand at him. "Oh, no worries. She's just my mother by blood."

He nods in agreement. He smiles. "Anyway, I had to do something, even though I knew I'd jeopardize my freedom. I wanted Lynn to go to jail. I was afraid she was going to hurt you."

I don't feel an ounce of love or admiration for Evan, despite his way of saving me. Because he knew what he was doing when Lynn hired him, and he has kept his secret from me for months.

The thought angers me. I fixate my eyes on him.

"Did you know Lynn was my mother?" anger rises inside of me, as I think that he must have known all along.

He nods, keeping his gaze down.

"Since when?" I press him further.

He looks up at me, his drooping with sadness. "I wasn't sure right away, but I was pretty certain she was when you first mentioned Jimmy."

"And you never bothered to tell me?" I raise my voice, and the guard behind me take a step forward, then stops.

Evan looks me in the eye and says, "I'm sorry I hurt you. You're nothing like them."

"That cold bitch really needed some serious help. Instead, she killed her husband." I continue. "There could have been so many alternatives to murder."

I shake my head, realizing who I'm preaching to. It's more like a monologue that doesn't need a listener.

"Anyway, thank you for confessing to the cops and bringing Jimmy's murder to justice. And for all the weed." A hollow laugh escapes me. "You know how you can be a puppeteer, holding the strings, but never appear on stage? All you need to do is move parts in the background, making sure the puppets do what you want them. Did Lynn once tell you about that last anonymous note, *RUN FOR YOUR LIFE?*"

He nods wordlessly.

"Yes—thought so. That's when all hell broke loose. I watched both Lynn and Jimmy falling apart, individually and as a couple. Jimmy drinking more and more, and Lynn getting more paranoid by the day and defending her territory. But when I send the note to Lynn to warn her about her life, she'd assumed Jimmy was after her." I can't help but smirk.

Evan stares at me, his mouth agape, and no words come out. I put the phone back, stand up, and blow him a kiss as I head for the door. The guard lets me out, and I exit, relieved I will never see him again.

As I walk, my thoughts extend further. Well, Jimmy *had* been after her, to be fair.

I'd watched Jimmy tamper with her car brakes with my own eyes.

Her paranoia by then was so strong that the only solution to that was preemptively killing Jimmy. Though I guess it isn't paranoia if someone really is out to kill you.

All staged by truly yours.

But shhh, don't tell anyone. Because when secrets begin to unveil, a slew of lies roll in. And why rock that boat now? This way, everyone gets what they deserve.

This was the last time I'd ever see Evan again. Or—excuse me—Skull.

Goodbye, sucker!

May both you and Lynn burn in hell. Jimmy is already there.

I COULDN'T SLEEP all night, anticipating the court's hearing. When I wake up, it's the same gray wall, the same bars across the wall facing me, and I wonder how many more years I'll have to stare at it. Today will decide my ultimate fate.

The guard opens my cell, and the keys jangling sound awaken my senses. He doesn't look at me and orders me to proceed through the door.

"Can I at least fix my hair first?" I comb fingers over my hair, and it feels like it's glued to my skull.

The least I can do is look somewhat decent, as I imagine everyone will be staring at me as I testify in court. In the jail, we're allowed to shower three times a week, but the last time I skipped, as I remained anchored to my spot in the cell, feeling lifeless. Now I regret that choice.

But the walls outside my cell are unkind. The women, those charged with a lesser offense, say, drug dealing or stealing, hate people like me. Everyone knows what each person is here for, and small cliques have been formed, hating on the other. For no other reason but false pride. Judgment. No matter what you do in life, killing another human is unforgiving. And if you don't believe in a God, your punishment will come as human punches or remorseless kicks in the shower.

"I'm afraid not," the guard says. He's a big man, a moustache on his fat face, thick dark brown hair. He looks like he hates his job, but perhaps he's just complacent. What the hell does he care about how I feel about my hair?

He leads me to the prison van and shoves me in the back, telling me to sit down. There are no windows except the barred one separating the driver and the space they put me in. I can't remember the distance between the Hampton jail and the courtroom. Even though it's been only two months, the town feels foreign, a faint memory in my mind, as if it's just an abstract notion. It's funny how the mind conjures and distorts images to survive. I wish I could see the town one more time, to remind myself of all the beautiful places and things I'd once enjoyed. The ocean breeze. The beach. Hell—even the shithole house I'd spent decades in seems like an object of my desires right now.

I crane my neck to peek through the bar window, but I can't see anything. The van takes a sharp turn, and I lose my balance and fall. Then it stops. We aren't moving again, and the door opens. The guard's face appears, telling me to stand up and move forward. I do it with difficulty, stranded by the handcuffs on my wrists and shackles on my ankles. He grabs me by the arm and pulls me toward him, telling me to jump out of the van.

He leads me through the back door of the courthouse, then down a narrow hallway where we finally enter the judgement room. As we enter, I gaze at the corner where the members of the jury are bulging their eyes at me, readying themselves to eat up my story like sharks in the ocean and spit out my ultimate destiny. Nick, my attorney, is already there and he stands up when he sees me.

The pews of the courtroom are filled with people, and my eyes dart all over until I see Lucy sitting in the corner. On her right side sits a man, holding her hand. That must be Fred. How nice of him to accompany her and be the emotional support. Lucy's face is nondescript. I can't tell what she's feeling or thinking. But I want to approach her and give her a hug, tell her I didn't mean for any of this to happen.

Shit—none of us means for any of the bad stuff to happen after the fact. After we face the consequences of our actions. We could now be a happy family if it wasn't for all my fears, paranoia, and doubts.

I regret the life I'd led, but there's no turning back. There's no chance to change anything.

The judge, an older man with eyeglasses and gray hair, looks at me, then gazes at the rest of the room and lowers his head to read from the paper. "Ladies and gentlemen of the court, esteemed counsel, and members of the jury, we gather here today to deliberate upon the case before us, the People versus Lynn Miller. The charges brought against the defendant are grave, and it is our solemn duty to sift through the evidence and testimonies to determine the truth."

I swallow.

"Lynn Miller stands accused of actions that strike at the very heart of our legal and moral code. The charges include the unlawful termination of a life and the conceal-ment of critical information pertaining to the demise of her husband, James Corrigan. As we embark on this legal jour-ney, it is imperative that we approach it with the utmost integrity and impartiality, recognizing the gravity of the allegations and the profound impact they have on the lives involved."

Everyone is charged with the anticipation. They are all ears, as the witnesses, one by one, come out to testify.

———

It doesn't take long to deliberate my sentence.

Half an hour after the hearing, we're summoned back into the courtroom and rise when the judge arrives. The collective whoosh motion as everyone gets up, then sits back down as instructed, is the only sound in the room. The judge is reading a note, containing what I assume is my sentence.

"Ladies and gentlemen of the jury, the time has come for you to fulfill the responsibility entrusted to you by the court. You have listened attentively to the evidence presented, heard the arguments of both the prosecution and the defense, and now stand as the arbiters of justice for the defendant, Lynn Miller."

A slight commotion is heard in the room. People shift in their seats, huffing and puffing, and clearing their throat. Then a dead silence.

A single jury member stands up, awaiting the question.

A third-degree murder. Forty years in prison without the chance of parole.

Whispers travel through the room, and the judge silences everyone, tapping his gavel against the wooden desk. I close my eyes. I will be in my nineties when my sentence is up. No chance in hell I'll survive until my day of freedom.

I wonder if Lucy will ever forgive me. I wonder if she will ever come visit me in the prison.

I gaze at the corner to look at her reaction to the sentence, but she is no longer there. I see Barbara in one pew, staring at me, and I think I see a smirk on her face. I'd expect to see Greta, my high school friend, but she isn't here. She must have given up on me. I don't blame her. All the other faces staring at me are unfamiliar, and I wonder if they are Jimmy's friends and acquaintances.

I draw my attention to a set of eyes staring at me, and I flinch when I see the familiar face in the last pew. His evil smile is unnerving, as if trying to further break me down. It's James. The cop who'd patrolled around my house ever since I moved in, attempting to reveal the mystery surrounding me. The motherfucker. I'm not surprised to see him here and I imagine he's satisfied now.

My throat tightens, but I stifle the feeling and put my head down. I can't look at anyone. I've betrayed everyone's trust and lied to their face.

The two guards drag me across the courtroom, with the shackles around my ankles, making a profound sound of confinement. I wish I could rewind my life and do it all over again. But in the absence of this possibility, I can only hope someone out there will learn a lesson from my life.

The guard shoves me into the van, with more might than the first time. Seconds later, the engine revs, and I head to my new forever home behind the bars. As the sun's brilliance intensifies, casting shadows through the window bars onto the van's floor, I contemplate the uncertain journey ahead, my gaze lingering on the fading world beyond the confines of these steel walls. Pondering the road ahead, I wonder if Lucy will ever come visit me. Will she ever forgive me? Will she ever call me "mother" again?

The answers to my questions elude me. But I hang onto the last glimpse of hope.

THANK YOU

I sincerely thank you for reading this book! If you enjoyed it, a positive review would mean the world to me.

Like other small-press and indie authors, I rely heavily on word-of-mouth recommendations to reach new readers. Please consider leaving a review, even if it's only a sentence, checking out my other books, and subscribing to my website. I'm also happy to answer any questions you may have, so do please get in touch with me via my website:

https://nadijamujagic.com

SUBSCRIBE

If you'd like to keep up to date with my latest releases, or get news about occasional free or discounted books, please sign up at the link below. We'll never share your email address and you can unsubscribe anytime:

https://nadijamujagic.com

A stranger, a murder, and a town on the brink
A Psychological Thriller
LORETTA
NADIJA MUJAGIC

Nadija Mujagić was born and raised in Sarajevo, Bosnia and Herzegovina, what used to be the former Yugoslavia back in the late 1970s. In 1997, she moved to the United States shortly after the end of the Bosnian War and has lived in Massachusetts since. In her spare time, she enjoys playing sports and electric bass guitar. *Lottery of Lies* is her eight book.

Non-fiction

Ten Thousand Shells and Counting: A Memoir

Immigrated: A Memoir

Fiction

Till a Better World: Women's Fiction

The Brilliant Mirage: A Thriller

The Exchange: A Psychological Thriller

The Master of Demise: A Psychological Thriller

The Nightmare Under the Mistletoe: A Christmas Thriller Novelette

Lottery of Secrets: A Psychological Thriller with a Shocking Twist (Book 1, Lottery series)